Also by Jon Howard Hall

Noccalula: Cherokee Princess of Alabama
A short story (available only as an e Book)

Kyzer's Destiny

Kyzer's Promise

Corporal Archer and the Siege of Vicksburg

A Place Called Winston

Simplicity 1834

Jennie Wade

and the
Gettysburg Affair

A Novel of Historical Fiction

Jon Howard Hall

iUniverse

JENNIE WADE AND THE GETTYSBURG AFFAIR
A NOVEL OF HISTORICAL FICTION

iUniverse books may be ordered through booksellers or by contacting:

iUniverse
1663 Liberty Drive
Bloomington, IN 47403
www.iuniverse.com
844-349-9409

ISBN: 978-1-6632-5978-3 (sc)
ISBN: 978-1-6632-5979-0 (e)

Library of Congress Control Number: 2024902931

Print information available on the last page.

iUniverse rev. date: 03/14/2024

Dedicated to the memory of all those who were wounded, maimed, or killed during the Battle of Gettysburg 1-3 July 1863.

Jennie Wade

and the
Gettysburg Affair

1863

Gettysburg, Pennsylvania

On the morning of 3 July, Jennie Wade never realized that her life was about to end within a matter of seconds. A stray bullet traveled through the kitchen door and hit her while she was kneading dough to bake bread that morning around 8:00 a.m. The bullet pierced her left shoulder blade, went through her heart, and ended up in her corset. She was killed instantly.

Mary Virginia Wade, born 21 May 1843, at age twenty is known to have been the only direct civilian casualty during the battle in Gettysburg.

The Gathering Storm

The Compromise of 1850 was established in the hope it would provide a permanent solution to the slavery controversy. Both major parties of the United States Government stood by the Compromise during the presidential election of 1852. Franklin Pierce, the Democrat, defeated the Whig candidate, General Winfield Scott, mainly because some northern Whigs were suspected of having abolitionist tendencies. There were businessmen, plantation owners, and Congressmen who joined in during this time to condemn those who kept bringing up the subject of slavery. However, the slave issue could not be suppressed.

The Fugitive Slave Law, which was part of the Compromise of 1850, held widespread opposition throughout the North. According to this law, the word alone of an owner of a runaway slave was to be taken as proof of ownership, while a suspected runaway had no right to testify in his own behalf. Most all of the state legislatures during this time passed personal liberty laws which practically nullified the Fugitive Slave Law. It simply forbade any state officials to assist in catching runaways. Northerners soon became less willing to tolerate slavery while Southerners grew more ardent in its defense. By 1851, the feeling of abolitionist sentiment in the South had nearly disappeared. It soon became almost impossible to free a slave in most southern states, while the fate of free Negroes grew much harder to contend with its outcome. A few southern states passed a law requiring free Negroes to choose whether to leave the state or return to slavery. Resolutions were passed by Georgia and South Carolina that if the North refused to protect all the rights of slaveholders, they would secede from the Union.

In 1854, the political truce over the

slavery issue resulted in the passage of the Kansas-Nebraska Act. This bill was pushed through Congress by Stephen A. Douglas, the Democratic Senator from Illinois. It stated that the region west of Iowa and Missouri be divided into two new territories, Nebraska and Kansas. The question of slavery in the new territories would now be left to the future decision of its inhabitants who would settle there as they moved into Kansas territory. It would become a race to see whether the majority of the settlers would come from the North or South. It soon came as no surprise that the results of the Kansas-Nebraska Act were disastrous. Many Northerners were aided by an abolitionist organization called the Emigrant Aid Society. This group supplied settlers with wagons, tools, livestock, machinery, and rifles. At the same time, a pro-slavery secret society, the Blue Lodge, dispatched armed men from Missouri into Kansas. Eventually, the struggle between the two factions reached the proportions of a civil war.

In the two years since the passage of the

Kansas-Nebraska Act, two new parties were established, the American and the Republican. The American party attempted to change the mindset of those who favored slavery by the diversion and strong feelings against the immigrants. Its candidate in 1856 was former president, Millard Fillmore. In the strongly organized Free states, the Republicans nominated the well-known popular hero, John C. Fremont. The Democrats, who followed the practice of dodging the slavery issue, chose as their candidate the Northerner from Pennsylvania, James Buchanan. The voting was clearly sectional, and the polling of the popular vote was denied the Democratic candidate; however, James Buchanan won the election with 174 electoral votes to become president in 1856.

In his inaugural address in March 1857, President Buchanan determined that the question of slavery in the territories be settled by the Supreme Court. Shortly afterward, the high court handed down what would be called the Dred Scott Decision. Dred Scott was a slave from Missouri who was taken by a former master into territory closed to slavery, and then brought back into Missouri. With financial support from Abolitionists, Scott sued for his freedom on the grounds that residence in free territory relieved him from slavery. On 6 March 1857, Chief Justice Taney upheld the Southern point of view that Dred Scott had no right to sue in a federal court because the founders of the United States did not intend Negroes to be citizens. Also, the Missouri Compromise that banned slavery had never been viewed as constitutional since the Congress had no right to prohibit slavery in the territories. Justice Taney argued that such a prohibition denied slaveholders their equal rights in the public domain. In the end, instead of solving the slavery dispute, the Dred Scott Decision made it extremely bitter. If the decision stood as law, the Republican Party may as well go out of existence since its stand was to keep slavery out of the territories which had been declared unconstitutional. Therefore, the Republicans claimed that the decision was not binding and should not carry any weight in the matter. On the other hand, Southerners called on the North to uphold the decision.

Now, the question of slavery in the territories spread into utter confusion over the final outcome of the Dred Scott ordeal. The decision was supported in the South, but was flatly opposed by the Republicans who were dominant in the North. The main question still lingered in everyone's mind while it became the main topic of discussion in the territory. Did the Dred Scott Decision forbid the people of a territory to decide whether they wanted slavery? This would become the most important issue in the Lincoln-Douglas debates of 1858.

Stephen A. Douglas and Abraham Lincoln became rival candidates for senator in Illinois. Douglas had served in the Senate for twelve years and was known as "the Little Giant" because of his small stature and great character appeal. He was the most prominent Democrat in Congress and hoped to be elected President in 1860.

Douglas was a short, thick-set, burly man,

having a large round head, heavy hair, and dark complexion with a fierce bull dog look. His total appearance radiated a sense of success. He usually dressed in a southern plantation style, while often wearing a nice broadcloth suit, clean linen shirt, and a broad-brimmed felt hat.

In contrast, Abraham Lincoln was the Republican candidate and was relatively unknown outside his own state. The height of Mr. Lincoln's political career had been a single term in the House of Representatives. He was a former Whig and was late in joining the Republican Party, although he was known as a clever lawyer and debater.

Lincoln was incredibly tall, angular, and somewhat awkward in his walk and gesture. He looked like something from the backwoods to most people. His trousers bagged at the knees and the sleeves of his coat barely reached his bony wrists. He usually wore a black stovepipe hat in which he stashed his important papers inside that only emphasized his gawkiness and gangly overall appearance. Abe Lincoln always seemed to be able to tell a good story and highlight it with a number of picturesque illustrations. His most outstanding characteristic was that he had a genius for clear and logical thinking. He followed the principles of the Declaration of Independence to the letter and was opposed to slavery. He wasn't an Abolitionist, and didn't plan to interfere with slavery in the southern states; however, he insisted that it be kept out of the territories. It was his thinking that if slavery was simply confined to its existing area that it might eventually die out. He also thought that to allow slave labor in the territories would make it harder for poor people to prosper.

Lincoln challenged Douglas to meet him in a series of public debates to discuss the main issues of the day in seven Illinois towns. The debates drew large crowds and their speeches received national publicity. In the first debate, Douglas made an attempt to show to the people gathered there in the town square just how he felt about the situation. He pointed out how he thought that Republicans in general, and in particular, that Lincoln himself were all Abolitionists bent on destroying the Union. When it became Lincoln's time to speak, he embarrassed Douglas by asking: "Is it lawful for the people of a territory to exclude slavery from their limits prior to the formation of a State Constitution?"

If Mr. Douglas answered in the affirmative with a "yes," he would support the principle of popular sovereignty, but would go against the Dred Scott Decision. This answer would improve his chances of getting re-elected as a state senator, but he would lose hope of any southern support for the Presidency in 1860. If he answered "no," he would deny the popular sovereignty on which he had based his political career, and would most likely lose the senatorial election.

To get himself out of this predicament, Douglas invented a formula known as the Freeport Doctrine. According to this, Douglas accepted the Dred Scott Decision which forbade Congress to bar slavery from the territories. On the other hand, he went on to point out that a territorial legislature could effectively discourage slavery by failing to pass the special regulations necessary to keep slaves under control. By his admission that a territorial legislature would practically nullify the Dred Scott Decision, Douglas won a narrow victory in the Illinois senatorial election at the price of losing the southern support for the Presidency in 1860.

While the anti-slavery sentiment continued, the nation kept drifting toward dis-union while the tension mounted throughout the territory. In October 1859, a fanatical slave named John Brown and his eighteen followers, led a raid and seized the federal arsenal at Harper's Ferry, Virginia. John Brown regarded himself as a self-appointed agent to free Negroes and punish slaveholders. His intention was to free and arm Negroes in the surrounding area to rise up against their masters, but the slaves refused to follow him. After ten of his men had been killed in the raid, Brown was captured. He was tried in a Virginia court for treason and murder, found guilty, and hanged in December. At his trial and execution, John Brown showed no sense of guilt, remorse, nor fear of death. Many Southerners regarded Brown's deed with horror while they feared nothing so much as a slave insurrection, and left to wonder if they would be killed in their sleep. Further shock came when it turned out that John Brown had been financed by northern abolitionists and that many of them regarded him as a martyr to the cause of human freedom.

While the election of 1860 approached, the Democratic Party split over the slavery issue. The northern wing nominated Stephen A. Douglas while the southern wing nominated John C. Breckinridge of Kentucky. A third group calling themselves the Constitutional Union Party, composed mostly of former Whigs, chose as their candidate, John Bell of Tennessee. With such a division in the Democratic Party, this opened the door for an expected Republican victory. Although receiving a minority of the popular vote, Lincoln won the electoral vote, and was declared President of the United States in 1860.

During the period between Lincoln's election

in November 1860 and his inauguration in March 1861, the following seven states seceded from the Union: South Carolina, Georgia, Florida, Alabama, Mississippi, Louisiana, and Texas. In February, delegates from each of these states met in Montgomery, Alabama, and formed a new union named the Confederate States of America while calling for the other slave states to join them.

At this time, there were two fortresses still in Federal hands: Fort Pickens in Florida and Fort Sumter, located on an island in the harbor of Charleston, South Carolina. When Lincoln heard that Fort Sumter was running short of supplies, against the advice of his cabinet, the President decided to send a relief expedition to them where they would not be forced to surrender.

Meanwhile, the newly elected President of the Confederacy, Jefferson Davis, had been struggling with the problem of withdrawing from the Union without fighting a war with the northern states. After he heard about the relief being sent to Fort Sumter, he authorized the military forces in Charleston into action. The shore batteries opened fire on the fortress on 12 April 1861, and following after forty hours of bombardment, Fort Sumter surrendered, and the civil war began.

By the summer of 1863, it had moved into a little town in Pennsylvania called Gettysburg.

Jennie Wade

Mary Virginia Wade, "Ginnie," was born at home in Gettysburg, Adams County, Pennsylvania, on 21 May 1843. Her father, James Wade Sr., was from James City, Virginia, while her mother, Mary Ann Filby, was from York, Pennsylvania. They met and were married on 15 April 1840 in Gettysburg.

Virginia had an older sister named Georgia Anna and three younger brothers who were called John James, Samuel Swan, and Harry Marion. Martha Margaret was her eldest sister that died at age four months in 1841. The Wade family lived in a rented house on Baltimore Street where James Wade ran his tailoring shop located on the south side of the residence owned by Mr. John Pfoutz. Mary Virginia was immediately nicknamed "Ginnie," but as she grew older, her family and friends called her Jennie.

Prior to 1850, James and Mary Wade built one of the first houses on Breckenridge Street when the population of their little town was only 2,400 inhabitants. The Wade family name would soon become well-known in Gettysburg according to the Adams Sentinel newspaper issue of 2 September 1850 when Jennie's father was arrested.

James Wade Sr. stood accused of stealing three hundred dollars from local resident Samuel Durborow after the cash supposedly dropped from his coat pocket during a business transaction. Wade fled to Maryland where he made his attempt to escape, but was quickly apprehended by Constable Weaver and Mr. Durborow who followed and tracked down the alleged thief. After his capture, James Wade was arrested in Washington City with a portion of the stolen money found to be in his possession. A week later, he was extradited from Washington and indicted for larceny in the case of the missing money of Samuel Duborow in Gettysburg. On 25 November, Wade was sentenced by Judge Joel B. Danner to two years of solitary confinement at Eastern Penitentiary. After his release, James Wade was found to be in a state of declining health with a questionable mental state. In January 1852, Mary Wade petitioned the Adams County Court of Common Pleas to have her husband declared insane. He was later committed to the Adams County Alms House, called the poor house, located to the north of Gettysburg. James Wade would remain there for the rest of his life. Now, the sole financial burden fell on Mrs. Wade and her two daughters while they became seamstresses to provide an income for themselves and the three boys.

During the next ten years, it was a struggle for the mother and her two young daughters, but together they managed to sustain a decent living for themselves. On her parent's wedding anniversary, Georgia Wade married John Louis McClellan in Gettysburg on 15 April 1862. Pvt. McClellan was presently serving as an enlisted man in the 2ⁿᵈ Pennsylvania Infantry Regiment, and the couple married quickly while he was home on a brief furlough. After Louis headed back to camp, Georgia moved into a rented duplex house on Baltimore Street located close to Cemetery Hill. With her sister now married and away from home, Georgia's move and absence created more difficulty for nineteen year old Jennie and her mother, Mary. At first, it was a struggle, but soon their work as excellent seamstresses kept them busy each day while they earned their livelihood serving the residents of Gettysburg.

"Jennie, have you finished the dress for Mrs. Grantham? She is here to collect it," Mary Wade called out from the front parlor.

"Yes, Mama, I will bring it there in just a moment," Jennie answered from the back room.

In a few minutes, Jennie stood in the doorway with a blue velvet dress draped over her left arm. Her dark brown hair was brushed and neatly piled up on her head while her hazel eyes sparkled as she greeted Mrs. Grantham with her usual warm and friendly smile.

"Good afternoon, madam. I hope you will be pleased with my work on the alterations I've completed for you. Do you wish to try on the dress and check the hemline?"

"No, dear, I trust your fine stitching as always, so that won't be necessary. I must say, Miss Jennie, you are looking radiant today. May I ask if you are still seeing that nice looking young man?"

"Not for some time, Mrs. Grantham. Jack has gone off to the war. I believe he is presently somewhere in Virginia."

"This war is a terrible thing, and I thought it would be over with by now," she replied. "I have a young son who is wanting to enlist, and he is only seventeen. His father and I are at odds over the matter, and I can hardly bear the thought of his leaving home."

"At least, my boys are much too young to even consider such a thing," said Mary Wade while she took the garment from Jennie in order to fold and present it to Olivia Grantham.

"Mary, would you please credit my account

for the dress and I will be back next week to make payment?"

"Yes, Olivia, by all means, and I will look forward to seeing you then. Have a pleasant afternoon, dear."

The elegant Mrs. Grantham gave a slight nod while she gathered her new formal dress and made her exit through the front door. Mary and Jennie took their seats and continued with the work at hand while a burst of sunshine spread its rays through the window of the room.

A disturbance by one of her sons in the next room sent Mary Wade immediately to investigate while leaving Jennie alone as she momentarily stopped her sewing. Jennie's thoughts turned to Jack while she pulled his worn photograph from her apron pocket. She felt along its rough edges while she gazed upon his handsome face.

Johnston Hastings Skelly Jr. had been a childhood friend of Jennie's since their early school days. Jack had an older brother named Charles Edwin Skelly and a best friend, John Wesley Culp, who were also well-acquainted with Miss Jennie. Jack, John, and Jennie had survived their childhood illnesses of the mumps, measles, and chicken pox, along with a few broken bones for the boys and a brief encounter of head lice for Jennie. While the three friends grew into their teens, it became evident that Jennie fancied Jack over John Wesley as a more favorable boyfriend. Her new found interest in Jack suddenly grew into a feeling of true love for him. It was her hope that one day Jack would realize this and return the same feeling and affection for her. Surprisingly, that had just recently happened when Jack made his promise by giving her his heart and tintype before leaving for the war. Jennie prayed for Jack every day while she waited for the war to end and his safe return home to Gettysburg. He had not made his proposal yet, but it was her hope that Jack would marry her someday.

Jack Skelly, a tall, lean twenty year old, had shoulder length brown hair and blue eyes, along with his muscular build and handsome face. Jennie loved his radiant smile, wit, and charming personality. How she missed being with him nowadays while he was away. Jennie's best friend, Maren Bathurst, already had the two of them engaged to be married by year's end, if her prediction came true. Maren viewed Jack and Jennie as a perfect match, always in hopes that Jennie would ask her to be maid of honor at their wedding.

Jack's father, Johnston Skelly Sr., had hopes of his son following his profession as a tailor, but young Jack had already become a successful granite cutter and stonemason in his own right. He worked regularly in and around Gettysburg, even when his father's work wasn't always steady. Jack had plans of operating his own business when he returned home, and maybe even get married.

Mary Wade's return to the room suddenly awoke Jennie from her daydreaming about Jack. She hurriedly slipped Jack's photograph back into her apron pocket.

"Thinking about that poor boy again?" Mary Wade returned to her seat beside Jennie and took up her sewing once again. "Girl, you need to pick yourself up and out of the doldrums because there ain't nothin' you can do about it 'til that boy comes back home."

"Yes, Mama, but I love him so, and pray for his safe return."

"I know, dear, it seems that the womenfolk are the ones who do all the worrying. Would you pass me that spool of blue thread?"

Jennie couldn't help but remember that it was during the winter of 1861-62, when the civil war was only seven months old, that she befriended a young corporal from New York. The 10th New York Calvary Regiment, also known as the Porter Guards, were briefly stationed in Gettysburg for three months. Several of the men, who spent their long wintry days drilling and perfecting the use of their sabers and small arms, eventually became regular customers of Mrs. Wade and her daughters. The Porter Guards had been dispatched to the little town in order to protect the state borders against any possible Southern intrusion. The Wade women were highly respected and perceived to be very kind and hospitable by the soldiers who used their services of uniform repair and various other jobs that required sewing or stitching. Jennie would always remember the day she met the young corporal who came into the shop with two of his friends.

"Yahoo! Anyone here?" yelled out the corporal as he entered the Wade house with his friends.

"I'll be there directly, sir," replied the friendly voice coming from the adjoining room. Jennie was smiling as she came through the doorway while her arms held tight around the three bolts of material and nearly dropped while she accidentally brushed against the hook mounted on the back of the door.

In a quick response, seeing the young lady's predicament, the soldier rushed forward in time to assist and prevent the load from dropping onto the floor.

"Here, let me help you," said the corporal while he took the three bolts from her and placed the cloth on a nearby table.

"Thank you, sir! I should have realized that my load was a little too heavy. Good morning, corporal. I'm Jennie Wade. How may I help you?"

"Good morning, Miss Wade! I'm Corporal Heath Callahan from New York and these two goons with me are Lt. Jacob Lancaster and Pvt. Harold Burkhalter. Jake and Harry are my two best friends. Well, ma'am, I guess I'm the one who is in desperate need of your services."

"It's nice to make your acquaintance, gentlemen. So, Corporal, how may I assist you?" Jennie asked while she quickly looked over the three young men.

Heath Callahan quickly caught her attention while she focused on the tall young corporal with the sandy blond hair and handsome face with his boyish grin and dimple in his chin. Heath's bright blue eyes held her attention while he faced her as his long arms moved to his backside and the seat of his britches.

"I'm afraid that I've had a little accident, Miss Jennie. You see, I've ripped out the seat of my pants and now have only half an hour to be present at my morning drill. There is no time to change my uniform. Can you please stitch me up?"

"Show me," she said.

In haste, Corporal Callahan removed his jacket and turned around for Jennie to catch a glimpse of two rosy pink cheeks peering from underneath the frayed woolen fabric, revealed in its rare form, perfectly round and firm. She took a quick glance and turned her head while Heath, in his embarrassment, now recalled his neglect in wearing any drawers today.

"My, my, Mr. Callahan, it does seem that you have caught yourself in a bit of a draft," Jennie said while she began to look for a needle and thread. "Go behind the screen over there in the corner, slip off your pants, and hand them to me. This will be a quick fix. Don't be shy, Corporal. I have brothers, so I am not surprised if I should see a young man's naked behind."

Corporal Callahan did as he was instructed and after a ten minute wait behind the screen, Jennie had his pants stitched and ready to wear while she placed them over the top of the screen. While she waited on the corporal to dress, Jennie tried to engage his two friends in pleasant conversation.

"Lt. Lancaster, now that the Porter Guards are spread throughout the city, what impresses you about our little town?" asked Jennie while she questioned the tall, black headed soldier with the thin moustache who stood closest to her.

"Gettysburg is a quaint little town, nothing like the big city I'm from in New York," he answered.

"What about you, Pvt. Burkhalter?" she asked the red haired, freckle faced young boy whom she perceived to be about seventeen.

"The townspeople seem to be very friendly for the most part, especially Mrs. Michaels who runs the bake shop. She's really nice!"

"Oh, yes," Jennie replied, "the widow Sarah is one of my mother's dearest friends."

"Well, looks as if I'm all stitched up and ready to go," said the corporal as he stepped from behind the screen. "Thank you, Miss Wade. You have saved me from receiving a demerit for improper dress. How much do I owe you for this speedy service? I am most grateful."

"There is no charge, Corporal Callahan. It was a simple fix. Just tell your friends about us should they need any kind of alteration. That will serve nicely as your payment."

He flashed a broad grin back at her while revealing an almost perfect set of pearly white teeth. "Your prompt and courteous service has most certainly rescued me today and I am most appreciative. Please accept a dollar from me, won't you?"

"Thank you, sir. I will put it toward the cost of supplies," she answered.

"You boys, ready to go? Good day, ma'am!" Corporal Callahan said while the three soldiers took their leave and he turned back in the doorway for a quick glance toward Miss Jennie.

Jennie remained alone in the shop for what may have been almost an hour without any customers. She took a seat on the window box and peered across Breckenridge Street while her eye caught a glimpse of a young soldier looking back at her. At first glance, the young man looked amazingly like Jack. The next moment, he was gone while Jennie pressed her face closer to the window pane. Her heart began to beat a little faster as she reclined against the window frame and let her mind wander back to the last night she spent with Jack Skelly.

Jennie remembered telling her mother, Mary, that she would be spending the night with Georgia after supper when she would walk to her sister's house on Baltimore Street by herself. That wasn't entirely a total lie, but first she had planned to meet the man she thought she loved, long before she was expected at Georgia's house for the night. Jennie gave no thought as to what her mother and sister might think about her meeting the Skelly boy that night; however, she knew all too well what could happen to her when she was finally alone with Jack. At this moment, she felt willing to do anything to spend this time with him before he left to go to war. Dark couldn't come soon enough while she hurried to the place they had agreed to meet.

The light from a full moon lit her path while Jennie observed the twinkling stars as they sparkled in the clear night above while she made her way toward York Street. She had planned to meet Jack in the gazebo beside the St. James Lutheran Church where she had been confirmed. Her heart was racing as she made her approach while pulling her shawl a bit tighter around her in the cool of the night. Jack was already waiting there as he stood to meet Jennie in the moon light.

"I wasn't sure that you would be able to come here tonight," he said while Jack gently took Jennie's hand and led her to a seat on an old wooden bench.

"Sorry that I'm a little late, but I had to finish all my chores before I could leave," she replied. "My dear mother and sister do not know that I planned to see you tonight."

"I wanted to come see you at your home today, but just couldn't get away. The 8th Corps Infantry is packing up to leave for Virginia early in the morning," Jack said while he reached to draw himself closer to her.

"I didn't realize that it was to be so soon,"

Jennie replied while she leaned against his chest.

"Me, either Jennie. The order came early yesterday morning, so this will be my last time to see you before I can return home after the war is over."

"I can hardly bear the thought of you having to leave, but I know you must. I'm going to miss you, terribly."

"Don't fret, Jennie. I feel that it will all be over soon, and I will be back home once again."

"Jack, what about our plans? When will you tell my mother about your intentions?"

"We'll just keep that our secret for now, don't you agree? I promise to talk to her as soon as I return. Just keep everything to yourself for now, and wait. Will you wait for me, Jennie?"

"You know I will, my darling!" she exclaimed.

"I was sorry to hear the latest news about our friend Wes Culp."

"What news?" she asked. "I haven't seen John Wesley in quite some time."

"That boy has up and joined the Confederate army to the shock of his brother William as well as myself. No one seems to understand why he would do such a thing."

"Nor I," she replied while her shawl dropped from her shoulders. "Sometimes, I believe that a man, and also a woman, must step out in faith and do whatever they think best for them at the time. Wouldn't you agree?"

"Yes, but to strictly go beyond the loyalty of family and friends, not to mention our town and the great state of Pennsylvania."

"That's his decision, Jack," she emphasized. "Do not let it bother you. You have chosen yourself to fight for what you believe in. I just pray that God will keep you safe and protect you from all harm while you're away from me, my love."

Jack drew her close and gave Jennie a passionate kiss on the mouth. Her waiting lips were full like a perfectly ripened peach, while her eyes began to moisten as a tear rolled down her cheek. Jennie moved her body to give Jack complete access to whatever he desired of her, but he resigned himself to suppress his sexual feelings with a gentle caress while he pulled away from her.

"Don't you want me?" she asked.

"More than you know, my darling, but we must wait and save ourselves for the day of our wedding. I couldn't bear to have you now, and then just leave you by the morning light."

"I am taken by the respect that you always show to me, but I am willing…"

"Say no more, Jennie. I want to remember you just as you are, pure in heart and mind, and so very beautiful."

"You flatter me, Jack Skelly!"

"No, I just simply love you, Jennie Wade. People all over this town love and respect you. When we are married, I want us to walk down the street and hear people say, 'Just look at her! There goes Mrs. Jack Skelly, such a fine and remarkable young lady.'"

"Now, you say no more, I'm blushing, Mr. Skelly."

"I must leave in haste now to return to camp before curfew, Jennie. May I walk you to your sister's house?"

"No, sweetheart! I want to remember us parting tonight in the gazebo."

The two young lovers kissed and embraced until Jack turned to walk away. Jennie stood there feeling helpless while she watched Jack Skelly disappear into the darkness of the night. In one brief moment, he was gone.

3

The Gettysburg Affair

By the time the summer solstice reached 15 June, Federal troops were completely surrounded while fighting broke out near Carter's Woods. This skirmish pitted Jack Skelly and William Culp against friend and brother, John Wesley Culp; however, this was unknown to each of them at the time.

While the fighting came close to its end, William Culp managed to escape. Not so lucky for Corporal Jack Skelly and his two sergeants, Ziegler and Holtzworth, who among all the others were captured and taken prisoner. As the action came to a halt, Skelly and several others were called upon to surrender their arms and fall to their knees. Taking the only chance that he thought he had, Jack broke away in a run back into the woods while he tried to escape. Shots rang out and Corporal Skelly was struck in the upper arm and back with a blast from a minie ball that stopped him cold. He fell to the ground in much pain while he was forced to surrender to his captors. While the victory march of the Confederate force, Johnson's Division of Ewell's Corps, continued their celebration, they passed by the prisoners gathered nearby. It was at that moment that Sgt. Holtzworth heard a familiar voice that greeted him in complete surprise.

"Hello, it's you," said the young man who made his approach in front of the sergeant who stood among a small group of Union prisoners. His voice seemed to be somewhat sympathetic with no malice toward his friend from Gettysburg. It was by complete surprise when Sgt. Holtzworth recognized the young man in the Confederate uniform.

"Hello, yourself," he called out. "I can't believe that I'm standing in front of Pvt. Wesley Culp."

"I thought that was you, Sgt. Holtzworth, while I was about to pass by," he said.

"Wes, your best friend needs your help immediately!"

"Who would that be, sergeant? My best friend is Jack Skelly and he's in Virginia, the last news I heard about his whereabouts."

"No, he's here right now, and he's been shot. You need to find him and see if you can get him some help as soon as possible."

"I will, sergeant, and thanks for telling me about him. We are sworn enemies on the battlefield, all of us, but lifelong friends back home. I regret that you and others from Gettysburg have been captured, but at least, you are alive."

Within the hour, Wesley Culp had located his friend Jack while he found him laying on a makeshift bed roll near the edge of the woods. All around the area lay a large group of men who were wounded or dead as Pvt. Culp's search ended as he fell to the ground beside Jack. Seeing that his friend had suffered so much pain and anguish, Wesley immediately sought out all he knew to do to quickly get help for him.

Jack lay before him in an unconscious state with his left shoulder bandaged while a soiled dressing revealed the flow that oozed from the already dried blood. He knew that time was of the essence, and if he couldn't get further help, then Jack would possibly bleed to death. By what seemed as a divine intervention, Wes Culp was able to get Jack loaded onto a wagon headed for a field hospital in the town. Culp hated to see Skelly in this condition, but he had done all he could do for him. And now, his own marching orders were to move out immediately, so he was forced to vacate the area with his company, thus leaving Jack behind.

Sometime later, possibly within the next few days, Wesley Culp was able to visit Jack in the Taylor House hospital where the doctor there gave him little hope concerning Jack's recovery. When Culp left Skelly that day, it was the last time they would ever meet.

During the many changing events now taking place in town, Jennie heard most of the rumors spread by the neighbors around her. Much like everyone else, Jennie and her family never considered fleeing the town. Instead, whatever was destined to happen in the coming days would now definitely seal their fate.

On 20 June, a telegram was sent to the townspeople of Gettysburg by Governor Andrew W. Curtin. Its message advised all residents to move their stores and possessions to a more secure location as quickly as possible, and seek their own protection. This frightened a great number of citizens who found themselves with no place to go, and caused somewhat of a frenzy, especially to the elderly and physically infirmed. All many of the people could do was to hope and pray that all the rumors would prove untrue.

Six days later, on 26 June, Gettysburg came face to face with its worst fear.

Invasion!

Confederate General Jubal A. Early's men entered the city by the way of Chambersburg Street with the officers waving their swords and the troops firing their guns into the air.

This spectacle sent many residents below to their basement while many were left to peer out behind their window curtains in fright. As far as Jennie Wade was concerned, the arrival of the Rebels marked the beginning of what was to become of her and her family during the course of that unforgettable day and a long time afterward.

On that particular Friday, Mary Wade was staying at Georgia's house on Baltimore Street and caring for her daughter who had just given birth to her first child. The baby, named Lewis Kenneth McClellan, was delivered by the family doctor who had remained in town and was called to the McClellan house by mid-morning. The infant was born about half past two o'clock, just one hour prior to the initial invasion by the Confederacy. This event, the birth of her nephew, left Jennie in charge of the family home on Breckenridge Street which was located about three hundred yards north of town.

Jennie, who had just turned twenty years old in May, had many responsibilities in the

Wade household every day. Today, especially would be no exception. One of her biggest jobs was the total care of a six year old crippled boy who was boarded at the Wade house while his mother worked in another part of town. Mary Wade earned extra money from her while it fell to Jennie to take care of little Isaac Brinkerhoff, whom she dearly loved. She had so much love and compassion for the lad since he could not walk or care for himself. Along with Isaac, Jennie also had charge of her little brother Harry, who was eight. Their total care was very time consuming for Jennie, but she also had to work with her mother as a seamstress, as well as to help with the cooking and cleaning. No easy task for a young girl in love, but she would set aside her main duties to help out or lend a hand whenever the need would arise and she found out about it. Jennie had a true servant's heart and her strength, courage, and faith was about to be tested once again.

Earlier that same morning, Jennie's brother John, nicknamed Jack, called upon his sister to help him with his uniform. Now, at age seventeen, he had enlisted in Company B of the 21st Pennsylvania Cavalry Regiment only three days ago, and had been assigned as a bugler. Jack was small for his age and stood only five feet three inches tall. When he received his uniform, it was two sizes too big, so Jennie was able to assist her brother by completing all the necessary alterations to it. Jack was grateful for her help, and Jennie was more than happy to fit him properly into his new Union uniform.

Jack's regiment, Company B, had been ordered to leave that day for scouting duty in southern Pennsylvania by way of the York Road, only a few hours before the Confederates would be arriving from the opposite direction. The young bugler was running late and missed leaving town with his regiment so Jennie helped her brother once again. They hurriedly packed his gear onto his horse, and said their fond goodbyes, while she watched him ride out alone to catch up with his company. In haste, Jack never had a chance to say goodbye to his mother, who was nearby at Georgia's house that day. All this seemed to happen so fast; a wave from horseback and the sight of a young boy heading out to the unknown, now appeared only as a faded memory since this brother and sister would never cross paths again.

Jennie's middle brother, Samuel, age twelve, lived and worked as a delivery boy for James Pierce, who was a butcher in his shop at the end of Breckenridge Street. Samuel was enlisted as a member of the Gettysburg Zouaves, along with his employer Mr. Pierce, who helped with his induction into the semi-military organization. When Pierce first heard about the Rebels soon to arrive in town, he instructed Samuel to take his favorite horse and ride out to the Baltimore Pike for safety and hide the animal. It was becoming known that the Rebs were confiscating all the serviceable livestock from the town, including any chickens and turkeys that they found running loose. Young Sam did as he was told while he quickly mounted up and rode toward the outskirts of town on his way to the pike. He no more got to the edge of town when he was overtaken by a small band of enemy soldiers who arrested him and led him back into town.

His sister, Jennie, happened to be standing near the corner of Breckenridge and Baltimore Streets when she learned that her brother had been taken captive while she witnessed him being loaded onto a wagon. She quickly ran toward his captors and begged them to let him go since he was just a child. When Jennie failed to convince the men who held him to release her brother, she hurriedly ran to the McClellan residence where her mother had gone to attend to her sister. Not wanting to disturb Georgia, Jennie called her mother out of the house to explain to her what had just happened to Samuel. It was almost four o'clock that afternoon whenever Mary Wade was free to go to the town square and appear before General Early and successfully secure the release of her boy. However, James Pierce's prized horse was retained by the Confederates. Samuel Wade returned to the Pierce house where he would spend the remainder of the upcoming battle downstairs in the basement. As the busy day's events drew to a close, Jennie Wade returned to her house to prepare a supper meal for little Isaac, Harry, and herself.

The next morning, General Jubal A. Early's Division departed from Gettysburg while the residents felt a brief time of relief. To many people, it felt as if a great swarm of locusts had invaded the fields and destroyed their crops. The overnight occupation certainly made the townspeople realize now what they were up against and what they might possibly experience on a much larger scale during the upcoming days. While sudden fear and alarm continued to rise, many able-bodied citizens sought ways to protect their property and themselves against a return of the Confederate invaders. There was not much that could be done to hide or shield the animals scattered all through the town. The dogs, cats, chickens, turkeys, sheep, goats, and cows were left in their pens and stalls; however, some of the horses were taken into the woods or down by the river to hide since they proved more easily to be moved. They were considered a great bounty if they were to fall into the hands of the enemy.

Several friends and neighbors shared their plans with each other during the next three days while the town continued with their preparation.

"I have stitched my gold wedding ring into the sleeve of my blue calico dress." *Mrs. Dorothea Wilkins (Breckenridge Street resident)*

"I have sewn my mother's heirloom brooch and all my other valuable jewelry into the hem of my daughter's dresses." *Adaline McKenzie (Baltimore Street resident)*

"I am moving a store of non-perishable foodstuffs into the loft of my hostelry on York Street."

"I also hid a supply of liquor in my garden underneath the cabbage patch." *Charles Wills (Proprietor of the Globe Hotel, York Street)*

"I assisted my father, Charles, in hiding sugar, ham, potatoes, and other groceries in our basement." *John Wills (Proprietor of the Globe Hotel)*

"I have stored my wife's silver service and

china hidden away in our attic." *Mr. James A. Rosencrans (Baltimore Street resident)*

"I leased an entire freight car and shipped a load of goods to a relative in Philadelphia." *James. F. Fahnestock (York Street resident)*

"I took my horses to hide in the woods near the pike." *Leonard H. Gardner (Chambersburg Street resident)*

So, on and on it continued while the town braced themselves against what was about to unfold. On Monday, 29 June, it was reported that nearly 13,000 Confederate troops were camped only a few miles from town. By nightfall, flickers from their campfires could be seen spread along the eastern slope of the mountain, only nine miles to the west,

By early evening the next day, 30 June, the first Northern soldiers appeared in Gettysburg in search of Lee's army who were reportedly camped nearby. These Calvary men were from General John Buford's Division which had been ordered to the area by General John F. Reynolds, commander of the First Corps, Union Army of the Potomac. After a long and tiring ride, the Federal cavalry arrived in town along the southern route by way of the Emmitsburg Road. They were welcomed heartily by the loyal citizens who applauded and cheered them while they made their entrance. After posting pickets in the north and west of town, the horse soldiers went into bivouac at the farms of James McPherson, James J. Wills, and John Forney. The farmland was located north and west of the Lutheran Theological Seminary.

Later that afternoon, the armies were in place and waiting on their orders. Everything was quiet on the home front. While the darkness of night drew its curtain across the sky above Gettysburg, the residents settled down for their last night of peaceful sleep, unaware of what tomorrow would bring upon them.

The Gettysburg Affair was set to begin.

4

1 July 1863

While the morning mist still lingered from the night before, General Henry Heth's Division of the Confederacy made their advance toward town. This unit on the march consisted of 5,000 or 6,000 infantrymen who were approaching from the west. By eight o'clock in the morning, they encountered Buford's 3,000 horsemen posted along McPherson's Ridge located about one mile west of town near the Seminary. With the thundering sound of cannon fire that boomed, along with the scattered rifle and carbine fire filling the air, this became the initial early morning activity that would begin the three day Battle of Gettysburg.

Soon after the conflict began, shells from the western battery fully awoke the town by exploding noises both near and in the town. The flying projectiles and shell fragments sent many residents scrambling down into their basements or leaving their homes for other places of refuge. Jennie was immediately faced with a decision of what she must do in the wake of this present situation.

"Quickly now, Harry! Get yourself dressed while I attend to Isaac," ordered Jennie to her little brother. "We are going to Aunt Georgia's right away!"

"But sister, why do we have to go now? It's so early and I want to sleep," Harry asked while he rubbed his eyes.

"Don't question me, young man. You just do as I say. We need to leave this house immediately."

"What's all that noise outside? I want to go see what's happening out there."

"No, you don't! Just put on your clothes. I've about got Isaac ready, and I'm taking him to Mother right away. I will come back to get you, along with a few things, so you need to be dressed and ready to leave. Please, Harry, you need to mind me, especially right now."

"All right, but I really want to stay here," he replied.

Jennie threw herself into full emergency mode while she made the decision to leave her comfortable home on Breckenridge Street. She felt that her sister Georgia's house near Cemetery Hill would be a much safer place to be, although she also hated to have to leave her home. It was a real effort to get little Isaac Brinkerhoff ready to carry him in her arms all the way to Baltimore Street. She knew her mother would be worried and wouldn't leave her sister Georgia, so she picked up the little crippled boy and left, leaving Harry with a final warning to be ready when she returned. After Jennie left Isaac with her mother, within the hour she returned to get Harry, along with a few personal items and their clothes. After she locked the front door, and put the key into her dress pocket, she began to doubt whether the war would permit her to ever return home.

When Jennie returned once again to her

sister's house, which now provided shelter for herself, Mary Wade, Harry, Isaac, Georgia, and newborn Lewis Kenneth McClellan, she soon found herself overrun with so many household chores. It worried her that Mrs. Brinkerhoff would not know where everyone had gone when she arrived later at the Breckenridge house to find it empty. Surely, she would know to look for them at the McClellan house. That notion would have to wait because now Isaac was demanding her full attention by needing to use the chamber pot; Harry was constantly wanting to go outside and see the soldiers posted along the street; the baby kept crying; and her mother needed help in preparing all of the family something to eat. In the midst of all that, while trying to get everything settled down for the evening, suddenly there was a knock at the door and it was left for Jennie to answer. She hesitated for a moment, and then opened the door.

"Pardon me, Miss, but do you perhaps have a cup of water that I might have to drink?"

asked the young Union soldier who stood on the doorstep. "I am so very thirsty."

"Please, have a seat on the porch and I'll see what we can spare," Jennie said while she closed the door and went to draw a dipper of water from the pail which sat on the dry sink.

"Who was that?" her mother asked.

"It is a young soldier in a dirty blue uniform wanting a drink. I can tell that he looks very thirsty." Jennie answered.

"All right, give him a drink. There is a leftover biscuit from breakfast on the stove top."

Quickly, Jennie returned as she opened the door and stepped out onto the porch, while appearing before the young man who was propped against the brick wall of the house. In her dainty hands she carried a cup of cool water and a cold stale biscuit which she held out for the soldier.

"Thank you, Miss Wade, I am much obliged and regret that I cannot repay you for your kindness right at this moment."

Jennie stepped back in puzzlement while

she took a closer look at the tall, blue-eyed man with sandy blond hair and dimple in his chin.

"Do I know you? How do you know my name?" she asked.

"So, you don't recognize me? Surely, I haven't changed that much." He paused a moment while she continued to stare. "I apologize for all the dirt on my uniform at present, but a while back, I was privileged to meet you at a house on Breckenridge Street where you stitched up the seat of my pants. I am Corporal Heath Callahan."

"Oh, Corporal, I'm sorry that I didn't recognize you right away. You caught me off guard completely this time. How do you come to be back in this part of town?"

"First, I was surprised when you opened the door and I saw you standing there. I wasn't expecting to see you, but while I was waiting, I knew at once that you were Miss Jennie. I could never forget your kind face and warm friendly smile. To answer your question as to why I'm here, well, that may take a while. Do you have time for me to answer?"

"Not right this very minute because I have so much I need to be doing to help out with my family," she said with regret.

"I completely understand, Miss Wade. The Porter Guards have been dispatched back into town as a back-up unit, so I will be stationed close by. If you can find time and want to talk, just look for me on the street. It is a pleasure to see you again. Good day, ma'am, and I thank you once more for the water."

Within a couple of passing hours, Jennie caught a break for a few minutes when she spotted Corporal Callahan posted alone across the street while she peered from a kitchen window. She told her mother that she was going to the well to refill the pail, but instead she left the house to see the young corporal once again. Jennie approached him in silence while a snap from a twig under foot gave her away. He rose up from where he was seated, tipped his cap, and stood facing her.

"So, I'm guessing that you have a few minutes to talk," he said.

"Yes, Mr. Callahan, and then I must hurry back into the house."

"I believe you wanted to know why I'm back in town, is that right?"

"Yes, I do, if you don't mind telling me."

"Well, it's like this. After we were pulled from the town, two weeks ago the Porter Guards were ordered to aid in the formation of a defense line. The strategy behind this movement was to ward off the Confederate forces located nine miles away while the Rebs made their approach on the Emmitsburg Road. If you remember my two buddies, Jake and Harry, I am sorry to report that Jake was severely wounded in the shoulder and taken prisoner, and young Harry was shot and killed. I barely escaped while the Guard was ordered to retreat back into the woods. I feel fortunate to have survived, but saddened at the loss of my two good friends. Harry's folks are going to be devastated when they get the news about their only son."

"I'm so sorry, but happy that you made it out of there," Jennie said.

"Yeah, me too, and without a scratch!"

"What's happening here? Everyone is on edge, frightened, and worried about all the shelling and cannon fire all around us," she exclaimed.

"I'm afraid it's going to get a lot worse, Miss Jennie, and that's why we have been ordered to re-position our soldiers back in town. You and your family need to stay inside as much as you can right now. It is getting dangerous now to be anywhere outside."

"Thanks for the warning, and you stay safe as well. I must go now and draw more water. It was good to see you again, Corporal Callahan. Goodbye until we meet again."

It was during this same time on Seminary Ridge that hundreds of Union troops were in retreat and heading to the south side of town. This maneuver was caused by a break in the right flank which now was sending hordes of tired fighting men down through the town and straight toward the location of the McClellan house where Jennie was sheltered with her family. After a while, a good number of thirsty men were pounding on the door and begging for water. It wasn't long and Jennie was standing on the dusty road outside with her pail, and dipping cups of water for the many soldiers who waited in line. Her dress was soiled and drenched with sweat from the heat of the day while she worked until she was certain that all who waited had been given drink. She had almost created a path while she ran back and forth to the well to draw more water. From time to time, she would look to see if Corporal Callahan was near, but it was evident that now he was gone.

Between five and six o'clock that afternoon, new battle lines were being formed by both the Union and Confederate army. The Northern Army of the Potomac was being forced to retreat through town and take up new positions on Culp's Hill and Cemetery Hill. Unfortunately, this put the McClellan house directly into the crosshairs and within easy rifle range. At the time, the Wade family didn't have a clue about the present danger that encircled them on this hot July day.

It didn't take long for the inhabitants in this part of town to develop a sense of insecurity while they watched countless Union troops on the run through the streets and alleys to escape the pursuit of the rebel soldiers following them close behind. The once quiet and peaceful streets now erupted with the frantic noise of yelling and screaming with echoes of rifle fire nearby and the boom of cannons in the far distance.

"You good people of Gettysburg, remain in your houses and go down into your cellars or else you may be killed!" yelled a Union officer on horseback.

"Please don't leave us and abandon our families to the enemy," pleaded a woman standing at her open front door.

"Have mercy on us and save our children," cried an old man.

"I regret now that I chose to stay here. I should have gone to my sister's," shouted a young mother.

A rebel soldier burst into a house on

Baltimore Street and started up to the second floor when the mother yelled at the young man.

"I beg you, sir, please do not go up there! You will draw fire on this house full of defenseless women and children."

Without another word spoken, Sgt. Beauregard Dupree turned and left immediately while Mrs. Amanda Rutherford nearly fainted onto her couch.

At the corner where Baltimore Street intersected with the Emmitsburg Road, stood the Snyder's Wagon Hotel, owned and operated by Conrad and Catherine Snyder. About a hundred yards behind the hotel on the grounds was an orchard filled with large fruit trees. The entire area soon began to be filled with Union sharpshooters who took over the hotel and several houses. This new line of defense was being formed on the rise to engage the line of Confederate sharpshooters who were moving rapidly into position as well.

So far, the McClellan house had not been chosen to have its interior and exterior used as a firing position by either force, although its residents now had to remain trapped inside its walls. Jennie did her best to keep her mother, sister, and brother as calm as possible throughout the evening. Fortunately, earlier in the day, Mr. Brinkerhoff had finally located them and had taken little Isaac home to his mother. Jennie was relieved to know that the boy was safe and now back with his family.

Across Baltimore Street on the left side, about a hundred yards from the McClellan house, lived a tanner named John Rupp whose workshop was located at the rear of his house. He survived by simply hiding in the cellar unbeknownst to the rebels who took over the back of the house to move in their sharpshooters. From this particular vantage point, they were able to fire on the Union pickets all the way toward Solomon Welty's fence and beyond.

Soon, the Confederate forces occupied the land from the back of the Rupp house beyond the tannery, and leading toward most of the town. The layout of the land, consisting of its higher ground, proved advantageous to both Union and Confederate sharpshooters while the firing began and continued all afternoon until dark. At times, the riflemen would seem unmerciful while many men from both sides fell severely wounded or dead in the place where they once stood.

The Wade's abandoned house on Breckenridge Street had been taken over by the Confederates who had been posted in that particular part of town. The structures that surrounded the house itself provided a clear view of the Federal position on Cemetery Hill and along the Emmitsburg Road.

As the day was drawing to a close, the outnumbered Union forces, commanded by General George G. Meade, were finally overpowered and were presently scattered around Cemetery Hill seeking their defensive positions while the night was closing in. The McClellan house and the Wagon Hotel, along with several other houses, were situated on a curved arc within the new Union defensive line. Georgia's house sat dangerously about fifty yards to the east of the arc, while it posed an almost perfect location for the Union sharpshooters. Most all of the dwellings in this vicinity became secure hideouts for the Yankee marksmen while they fired on their Rebel counterparts, who were seen slinking in and out of buildings around the John Rupp Tannery site and other houses nearby in the area.

While night time continued to settle in the McClellan house, which Jennie had sought as a place of refuge, it became quite obvious that this might not be the best place to be after all. The Confederate sharpshooters who were stationed in the Rupp Tannery on the opposite side of the street began firing at Union pickets positioned around the little red brick duplex. The John Louis and Georgia McClellan house was now caught directly in the crossfire.

While the rifle fire continued until dark, the bullets riveted the area like a unrelenting hailstorm, and it wasn't long until a few Union soldiers fell mortally wounded within the McClellan yard and a nearby vacant lot. Still, Jennie Wade took the time, while she risked her own life, to go out into the yard to bring water and cheer to those men who lay wounded and dying.

Throughout the day, the women inside the house kept themselves busy, so there was not much time to be frightened. Georgia's bed had been taken downstairs to the parlor while the danger had increased since the early afternoon. At bed time, a fully-dressed Mary Wade reclined on the bed with her daughter Georgia and baby Lewis, while Jennie rested on a lounge under a window at the north side of the house. Harry slept in a trundle bed on the floor near the fireplace.

Around ten o'clock that night, most of the firing had stopped around the house, although the booms from the cannons across town could be heard and sometimes felt at any time. This made sleep almost impossible while the long day was ending with the cry and moan that was heard from the wounded soldiers outside in the yard.

5

2 July 1863

By morning's first light, the battle lines were drawn almost parallel while the main portions of both armies were positioned nearly one mile apart. The Union forces held Cemetery Ridge while the Confederates awaited their orders on Seminary Ridge to the west. At dawn, General Robert E. Lee ordered an attack against both Union flanks. Later that morning, Lt. General James Longstreet's attack on the left Union flank turned the base of Little Round Top into shambles, left the Wheatfield strewn with the wounded and dead, and overran the Peach Orchard. Thus, the Confederacy was first to jump start the second day of battle on this Thursday morning, while the rifle firing began once again ripping up and down Baltimore Street.

The bodies of the wounded and dead lay strewn along the street, porches, doorways, and alleys at the rising of the sun. A Union soldier stationed on the north side perimeter of the house, estimated that the structure had already sustained at least 150 bullets which penetrated the residence and grounds. So far, the house itself had not been the target of artillery; however, things inside were about to change for the Wade family and the McClain's who shared the other part of the two-sided dwelling.

Suddenly, the frequent sound of the bullets striking the outside walls were interrupted by the crash of a misdirected ten pounder Parrot shell, most likely fired from Oak Ridge about two miles away. The blast from the screaming shell burst through the slant of the roof over the stairway on the north side, passed through the wooden shingles, and penetrated the plaster wall upstairs. While the speeding projectile continued on its flight of destruction, it plowed itself into the brick wall on the south side of the house. The impact shook the place like an earthquake, while the shell finally came to rest above the exterior extension of the roof where it lodged itself and never exploded.

When she heard the crash of falling bricks, the splintering of wood, and plaster crumbling down from the walls and ceiling upstairs, Jennie fainted and fell onto the floor. A loud scream was heard on the other side of the house where Mrs. Catharine McClain lived with her four children. She huddled with them in her kitchen and prayed that their lives would be spared. Mary Wade, Harry, Georgia, and her baby were shaken, but all found to be okay following the blast.

"Help me to get Jennie onto the bed," cried out Mary Wade while she fell down at her daughter's side, along with Georgia, who herself was almost in shock. "Slip your hands under her shoulder while we lift and stand Jennie to her feet, and then move her to the bed," Mary added.

Young Harry was shaking underneath the bureau while baby Lewis fretfully began crying at the top of his lungs. Sudden panic had just struck the McClellan house. The two women settled Jennie onto the bed where she revived herself within the next few minutes.

"What just happened?" Jennie asked. "Why am I on the bed?"

"You fainted, dear," said her mother. "The house just took a hit from a shell, but thank God, it didn't explode!"

Georgia picked up her baby to try to calm him while she held the infant close in her arms. "Hush, hush my sweet boy! Mama's right here," whispered Georgia while she began to nurse six day old Lewis.

"We need to check upstairs," said Mary Wade.

"I'll go," said Jennie while she left the bed and headed toward the stairs.

Mary Wade reached down and pulled Harry from under his place of refuge. "It's okay to come out, son, we're all right just now. Jennie has gone upstairs to check the damage," Mary said.

"I'm scared, Mama," said Harry. "I want to

see my brothers. Will Jack be killed in the war and what about Sam?"

"I don't know, Harry. Hopefully, your brother Samuel will be safe right now in Mr. Pierce's cellar. I'm afraid all we can do for Jack is to pray for him wherever he is," said Mary Wade while she knew she must do something to help calm Harry. She reached for an apple in a pewter bowl on the table and handed it to young Harry.

"Come sit by me, Harry, and let me tell you a story that my father told me when I was about your age." Harry moved in closer, suddenly appearing more calm and relaxed.

The Story of Pocahontas

The two best things about Captain John Smith were, that he was never idle and he never gave up. He was considered to be a fair and good man while the colonists at Jamestown held him in high esteem. That means that they respected him and liked all the things he did. Captain Smith was always trying to find out something new or to accomplish some great thing he would discover. He never found a way to China on the Chickahominy River; instead, he only found a muddy swamp and eventually got himself captured by the Indians.

While Captain John Smith was a prisoner among the Indians of Powhatan's tribe, he met the chief's daughter, Pocahontas, a young maiden who became friendly toward him. At some point during his captivity, Chief Powhatan ordered that Captain Smith be put to death. When the Captain's head was laid upon the stones, and the Indians gathered around to beat out his brains with clubs, Pocahontas fell across him and placed her head on his. Powhatan realized that he could not have Captain Smith killed without first striking his daughter, so he let him live.

During this time, Pocahontas would sometimes travel from the Indian village to Jamestown, and when she found out that the settlers were in danger of starving, she brought them food. She also found out about a band of Indians among her people who were plotting to kill Captain Smith, and Pocahontas went to his tent at night to warn him of the danger. He offered her trinkets as a reward, but she tearfully refused them, saying that

Powhatan would kill her if he knew of her coming there. Later, when a number of white men slipped into Indian country and were captured and put to death, she saved one young man, named Henry Spelman, by helping him to escape.

When Captain Smith had lived in the colony for two years, ships came from England and brought hundreds of people to Jamestown in 1609. Several of the men were known to be enemies of the Captain, and when they learned that he had become the governor of the colony, they plotted against him to take control of the government. Captain Smith had recently been injured by an explosion of gunpowder, and he finally gave his consent to return to England after several charges were filed by those men who were his sworn enemies. One of the charges stated that he wished to marry Pocahontas in order to gain possession of the colony by claiming it for the daughter of Powhatan, whom the English regarded as a king.

There were many other people in the colony who became sorry that Captain Smith was to be sent away after Jamestown was taken over by a group of ruthless men. Chief Powhatan was no longer friendly, and Pocahontas stopped her visits into Jamestown. The people became afraid of the Indians and remained within the fortress of the town. It wasn't long and all of their food was gone, even to the point of having to eat their horses. Several people were killed by the Indians, while some escaped in one of the ships and became pirates. Many died in great numbers from hunger and starvation.

At last, other ships arrived to bring help to the colony. A new governor was appointed while Jamestown continued to suffer from sickness and trouble with the Indians. During this time, there was a sea captain named Argall who thought if he could get Pocahontas into his control, that Powhatan might be persuaded to live more peaceable with the colonists. Under the pretense of trading to her a copper kettle, Argall tricked the eighteen year old Pocahontas in coming with him to Jamestown, where he held her prisoner for a year. The colonists refused to give her up unless Powhatan returned some guns which the Indians had taken during one of their raids.

There was an Englishman living at the time in

Jamestown named John Rolfe, who fell in love with Pocahontas, and eventually proposed to marry her. When Chief Powhatan was sent word about the engagement, he readily agreed to the marriage. The uncle and two brothers of Pocahontas went down to Jamestown to attend the wedding. Pocahontas had been instructed in the Christian religion and was baptized when she married John Rolfe in 1614. Her real name was Matoax, but her father always called her Pocahontas. After she was baptized, she took the name of Rebecca. The marriage to Mr. Rolfe brought peace with the Indians for a while. In 1616, following the birth of a baby boy, John Rolfe took his family to England, where Pocahontas became known as the Lady Rebecca.

Before their voyage to England, some people in Jamestown told Pocahontas that Captain John Smith was dead, and she became greatly offended when she saw him alive in England upon their arrival. Soon after, she announced her intention of calling Captain Smith her father, after the Indian plan of adoption. As Mrs. John Rolfe, the Lady Rebecca was happy to live in England for a while, and became disappointed when her husband decided to return to Jamestown. By the time they planned to leave on another long sea voyage, Pocahontas contracted smallpox and died. Rolfe left his son in England with family relatives and set sail for America. After the boy was grown, young Rolfe sailed to Virginia in hopes of finding his father. Following the deaths of Pocahontas, and also her father, Powhatan, there were more Indian uprisings. In 1622, they attacked the settlement and killed more than three hundred people in one day. Long and bloody wars followed, but Jamestown somehow survived.

"Well, how did you like my story? You see, Harry, it's very similar to what we are going through right now in Gettysburg. Not everyone has the same mindset, and because of the many differences of opinion, our country has decided to go to war against itself to try and settle those differences. That's all I know, son. May God be with us all during these next days and keep us safe." Mary Wade tried to force a gentle smile while she reached down and hugged her boy.

Jennie returned downstairs to report her observance of the shell that she saw lodged in the rafters. "Let us also pray that the shell doesn't go off and k...." She caught what she was about to say while she glanced down where Harry huddled against his mother. "I see that the yeast has risen in the dough, so we need to busy ourselves and bake some more bread. Come with me, Harry, and you can help."

During the next hour or two, Jennie would go outside with water and slices of freshly baked bread to offer to the soldiers stationed near the house. The erratic firing in the neighborhood continued all during the day, and miraculously, there had been no injuries to the inhabitants of the McClain and McClellan house. Mary Wade gave up on trying to stop Jennie from going outside and putting herself in constant danger, while she tried to bring comfort to the men who lay around the house and in the yard. By late afternoon, Jennie continued baking bread, long after her mother stopped to help Georgia Anna with the baby. It was extremely hot in the house while the stove was kept fired up for baking. By night fall, Jennie and her mother realized they needed to start more yeast to be mixed into the dough where it could rise and be ready by early morning. As the women prepared themselves for another restless night, they lay down exhausted in their beds while trying to get a little sleep. Jennie would have been even more restless and upset if she had known that only a mile or so away, John Wesley Culp was camped within the Rebel defensive line. Her long-time friend could also possibly be carrying a message from Jack Skelly that was intended only for her; however, Jennie did not know these things.

On that night of 2 July, Wesley Culp obtained a pass to go into Gettysburg to visit his sister, Barbara Ann Culp Myers, who lived on West Middle Street. Located across the street from her, lived Johnston and Elizabeth Skelly, the parents of his best friend, Jack Skelly. Wes Culp found no one at home when he knocked on their front door. Unknown to him, the Skelly's were hiding in the cellar of their neighbor, Harvey Wattles, whose house was just down the street. The sound of rifle fire in the distance penetrated the night sky while the stocky, sun-bronzed, and weather-beaten young lad crossed the street. He was clad in the rusty, somewhat tattered butternut uniform of the Army of North Virginia as he reached the porch of his sister's house. He rapped boldly three times on the oversized front door made of oak. In a moment, the door was opened by a petite young lady with bright blue eyes and dark brown hair that was pulled up under a white lace cap. She appeared in the doorway wearing a pale blue cotton dressing gown and a light colored wrap that she pulled across her arms and shoulders. She seemed surprised at who would be calling at this time of night, unannounced and unexpected. There was a slight pause as the stranger was invited to enter and then a glad look of recognition as the sister clasped her arms around her younger brother. They hugged and he kissed her on the cheek.

"Why Wes, you're here! What a wonderful surprise. It's so good to see you again."

"Hello, sis. You're looking as pretty as always. How have you been?"

"I'm doing well, despite all these horrible conditions which are happening all around us. It's dangerous to be standing on this porch right now. Come in and have a seat," she said as she closed the door and pointed to a chair across the room.

"I'm probably a bit too dirty, and I certainly wouldn't want to soil your nice blue velvet chair."

"Nonsense, that old chair! Remember that was our Granddaddy Culp's, and I was just thinking yesterday that if the Rebs wanted to loot my house, they would never take that old chair. It's almost ready for the burn pile. Sit yourself down while I put on the tea kettle. The embers are still burning in the stove."

"Don't trouble yourself, my dear sister. I wouldn't care for anything to drink, and besides, I don't have that much time. I just wanted to come see you since I was close by."

"I'm so glad to see you now. It's been quite

a while, and I feel I must warn you, in case you don't already know."

"What's that, Annie? Tell me, sis."

"Well, I heard about some talk among the Culp relatives, saying that if they ever see that turncoat Rebel, they'd just as soon shoot him on the spot. I was horrified!"

"Yeah, I already heard about that. Don't worry your pretty face about it. I don't plan to see that side of the family anytime soon."

Annie pulled a small mahogany lady's chair near where Wes was sitting in order to be seated closer to him. She thought about how much he looked like their late father, while she wondered why Wes would choose to come see her now, and not their other sister, Julia.

"When have you last seen Julia?" she asked.

"I think it was during this past Christmas at our family gathering. How is our baby sister?"

"She's well. I believe she is staying over on York Street at our cousin's because her house has a cellar and Julia's small house does not have one. Are you planning to see her while you're in town?"

"Not right now. I don't have time, but you tell her I said hello and will try to see her as soon as I can."

"I know she would love to see you. In fact, she asks about you often, and all I can say is he's off somewhere in the Confederate army. Just between you and me, would you tell me why you suddenly joined up with them?"

"Well, Annie, as I remember I was about to join the Union forces, but one night I got a little wasted down at O'Hara's, and got into a big argument with a total stranger. Come to find out, he was a Reb and he dared me to join up and draw a big cash bonus in silver. The next thing I knew, I woke up the next morning with my orders stuffed into my pants pocket, along with two silver dollars. I never saw the man again, but I keep a sharp lookout for him. I want to tell him how all this has changed my life. The Confederacy isn't really so bad. I can see how they must feel about the issue of slavery. Now, it seems that we all have to pick a side, and go with what we believe is the right thing. Is that what they call Freedom?"

"Wes, I respect your service to the Confederacy, but understand that there are many who deem you as traitor. You could never do anything wrong in my eyes, and know that I will always love you, no matter what."

"I love you, too, sis. Now, I really need to go since I only have a two hour pass."

"Can't you stay until morning?"

"I'm really sorry I can't tonight, but I hope to come back in the morning. I almost forgot something very important."

"What's that, Wes?"

"While I was coming through Winchester recently, I ran across Billy Holtzworth who was a prisoner in our hands. He told me that Jack Skelly had been shot and wounded badly in the arm and shoulder, and had been taken to a field hospital where I found him that same day. Later, I was able to see him once again at the Taylor House hospital. He looked real bad, and couldn't talk very much. Jack gave me a message for his folks which I am to tell his mother. It is late now, and I didn't find them at home tonight when I knocked on their door.

You tell Mrs. Skelly I will come back in the morning and will you please have her here. I really need to talk with her."

"Is there no message from Jack for anybody else in Gettysburg, Wes?"

"Never mind. You'll get all the news once I tell Mrs. Skelly."

"I can give her a message tomorrow if you want."

"Naw, I need to deliver this message in person."

"You ought to stay the night here, Wes. Come back, brother. We may never see you again."

Wesley Culp made no response as he turned and walked away in the darkness. He returned to his company that night which was called the Stonewall Brigade, now commanded by General James A. Walker.

Wes Culp's sister, Annie, went to bed that night, but found she wasn't able to fall asleep so easily. Her brother was on her mind, and she couldn't seem to shake off a bad feeling.

6

3 July 1863

B y dawn's early light, the Stonewall Brigade made their bold attempt to seize the place, ironically, called Culp's Hill from the Union forces. Culp's Hill consisted of two rounded peaks, separated by a narrow saddle formation on the hillside. The eastern slope descended to Rock Creek while the western direction joined McKnight's Hill, formerly called Stevens Knoll, and was positioned 100 feet lower than the main Culp's Hill summit.

The hill was owned by a farmer named Henry Culp, and two of his nephews were brothers: John Wesley Culp, who joined the Confederate States Army in the 2nd Virginia Infantry; and William Culp, who was in the Union Army with the 87th Pennsylvania

Infantry. William was not present in Gettysburg during this time; however, it was known that he harbored ill feelings toward his brother Wesley by regarding him as a traitor and never speaking to him again.

Culp's Hill was a critical part of the Union Army's defensive line. The right flank formed its main position that featured the "barbed" portion described as the "fish-hook" line. Holding the hill by itself wasn't all that important because its heavily wooded area made it unsuitable for artillery placement; however, its loss would be felt as catastrophic to the Union Army. The importance of possessing the hill was that it dominated Cemetery Hill and the Baltimore Pike, while keeping the Union army supplied and blocking any Confederate advance toward Baltimore or Washington City. General Robert E. Lee's plan was to renew his previous attacks by coordinating a takeover on Culp's Hill with another attack by Longstreet and A.P. Hill against Cemetery Ridge. The skirmish, basically fought hand to hand, was very bloody with almost 2,000 losses on both sides.

It was nearing 8:00 a.m. when Wesley Culp took his position and moved up to the front line. The last thing he could possibly sense after being struck down and mortally wounded was the thought of not being able to deliver his message to Mrs. Skelly. It was the third day in July; it felt like it was going to be another hot one; and Wesley Culp lay dead in the dirt.

Almost four hours earlier, Jennie Wade awoke, completely unaware of the near proximity of Wesley Culp to her, let alone any message he might have for her from Jack Skelly. All she knew was the sun would be up soon, and there would be so much more to do around the house today, but mainly just to remain safe and survive the outcome of this war at all cost. It was sad for her to see all the death and destruction that was happening to the only home she had ever known. Jennie knew she must remain strong for her family and the man she loved. All she could do this morning as she rose from bed was to think about Jack and wonder where he was and how he was doing.

She prayed for his safety while she tied her hair back and walked into the kitchen.

Around 4:30 a.m. that morning, Jennie and Harry cautiously slipped outside to the wood pile to gather enough wood to bring inside and start up the stove. The dough, prepared from the previous night by Jennie, had risen nicely and looked ready for baking as soon as the oven was hot. Mary Wade was just waking up to find Georgia already up with baby Lewis. Jennie got the fire started and then returned to her lounge under the window to read the Bible and have her morning devotion by the light of a kerosene lamp sitting on a small table by her bed.

Jennie perhaps had no more thoughts on this particular morning than being right there in Gettysburg at that moment to serve those in need. Beside her mother, sister, brothers, and newborn nephew, there were three men now in her life that she really cared for: her eldest brother, her brother-in-law, and the man she truly loved. All three were serving on a battlefield somewhere unknown to her, but Jennie felt she had an opportunity to serve the wounded and hungry soldiers who crowded around her door step each day. She also felt that if she could give food, drink, or a comforting word to those in need, there may be a kind and gentle lady out there somewhere doing the same for the men she loved.

"Mama, please order Jennie to stop going out and giving away our bread and water to all those dying men. It's much too dangerous for her to keep going outside for any reason," Georgia complained to her mother while she passed Lewis over to her waiting arms.

"I've already mentioned that to her several times, while she seems to have turned a deaf ear to anything I've said for the past two days. That child has always had a mind of her own, so just let her be, Georgia. She thinks whatever she's doing is for the best."

"Well, Jennie could get herself killed right out there in the yard is all I know," Georgia said while Jennie overheard her sister's remarks as she entered the kitchen where the two stood talking and starting to prepare their meager breakfast.

"If there is anyone in this house today that is to be killed, I hope it's me since you, my dear sister, have a new baby," Jennie said while she strode past to check the fire in the stove.

While the rifle fire outside was beginning to start up once more, the three women and Harry huddled around the kitchen table for their breakfast of bread, butter, applesauce, and coffee.

Shortly after seven o'clock, all the windows on the north side of the house came under fire by the Rebel sharpshooters. Within a few seconds, all the panes were shattered while fragments of glass sprayed into the room and onto the heart pine floor. One stray bullet entered the front room, struck the bedpost, hit the wall, and fell onto the pillow at the foot of the bed where Georgia and her baby lay resting. They had moved there for safety measures at Jennie's suggestion since she thought that shots could easily come through the west door and windows at any time. The slug was still warm when Mary Wade picked it up from the bed, along with a few splinters of wood from the bedpost, which she gathered as a memento of what could have easily turned into something very tragic.

The clock on the mantel had just chimed eight times when Jennie stood from her chair and took her usual position in front of the dough board and tray. This had been her early morning duty for as long as she could remember. The dough tray was made of wood and was built somewhat like a small casket on legs with a hinged lid that served as a work surface where the flour and baking soda could be made into dough. The tray stood on four sturdy legs and when the lid was opened, the dough could be stored down in the box until ready to bake.

At 8:00 a.m. Jennie felt she was running late since she had promised a soldier last night that she would have a batch of biscuits ready baked early this Friday morning. Hurriedly, she sifted the flour, adding in the milk, soda, and shortening, and began kneading the mixture into dough. She had just dipped a little more flour onto her hands, and asked her mother nearby to check the oven, when a lone rifle shot rang out while it made its sudden entrance into the room.

The bullet had penetrated the outer door on the north side of the McClellan house, and also the door which stood opened between the parlor and the kitchen. It struck Jennie in the back below the left shoulder blade, pierced her heart, and embedded itself into the front of the corset she wore. Jennie's hands were still covered in flour and dough when she fell onto the floor. Jennie Wade was killed instantly that morning by a stray rifle bullet from an unknown assailant. How could this tragic event happen to such an innocent young lady?

Standing nearby, Mary Wade fell down to check her daughter's wound, only to determine the breath had left her body, there was no pulse, and sadly, she was gone. Mary Wade rose up and calmly walked into the parlor where Georgia sat with Lewis cradled in her arms.

"Georgia, your sister is dead!"

The screams from Georgia immediately alerted several soldiers stationed outside in the yard while they broke through the door and rushed into the house. They stumbled upon the body of the young girl lying dead on the kitchen floor, while Mary Wade and Georgia knelt beside her, while crying in deep anguish.

"My daughter, my precious daughter! They've killed her while she was making biscuits here inside the house," Mary said while she fell down into a nearby chair. Georgia pressed herself across the arm rest while she leaned against her mother's trembling body to try to bring comfort to her. Harry climbed into his mother's lap and started to cry.

After a quick examination of the body, the sergeant rose from the floor and stood before the two women while he removed his hat in their presence.

"I am Sgt. Jacob Hawthorne with the 10th New York Cavalry, Porter Guards, at your service, ma'am. And the deceased here, is this your daughter?"

"Yes, Sgt. Hawthorne," mumbled Mary Wade.

"I am truly sorry for your loss, ladies. May I assist you at this moment?"

"Yes, please. This is my sister, Jennie Wade. I am Georgia McClellan and this is our mother, Mary Wade. We are at a loss as to what to do next. I can't believe that this has happened."

"My men are checking the house. It looks as if a stray bullet came through the door on the north side of the house and struck Miss Jennie. I can assure you that she did not suffer as her death came quickly."

"What can we do now?" Georgia asked the sergeant.

"We need to get everyone moved to the other side of the house and out of the crossfire. It should be a bit safer there."

"I won't go, unless we can take my daughter's body," said Mary Wade.

"By all means, Mrs. Wade. I will see that my men safely transport Miss Jennie while we take leave of this side of the house. Gather what things you will need while I figure the best way we will be able to move," said Sgt. Hawthorne.

The Porter Guards quickly took charge after studying the present situation among themselves in a hurry-up discussion. The men gave final instruction to the women to get ready to go to their neighbor's cellar located on the opposite side of the double-dwelling. There was only one slight problem with this plan. How can this be accomplished with all the continual rifle fire going on outside?

To get there under normal conditions, one would simply have to walk outside toward the southern end of the house, and then descend through the outside cellar door. Presently, with the possible danger of taking a hit from the flying bullets, this was no longer considered an option. Soon, a young private discovered upstairs that the place where the shell had lodged itself the day before, could possibly become the way to escape safely. After kicking and tearing away the remaining plaster to enlarge the hole, enough space was created in order to get everyone to the other side without having to venture outside. The women were now instructed by Sgt. Hawthorne to climb the McClellan staircase, pass through the large opening, and walk down the other stairway on the McClain side of the house. From there, they could carefully slip outside through the kitchen door to the cellar entrance which was located only a few feet away. In the end, the shell that so dangerously came close to killing the Wade family the day before, now became their salvation by providing this interior route to safety while becoming undetectable by the Rebel marksmen.

Within the hour, the newly formed entourage was set to begin their trek to the other side. Without assistance, Georgia held her baby close while she ascended the stairs, followed by a soldier who carried a split-seat rocking chair. When she arrived at the top, she handed the infant to another soldier before she entered the opening. She crossed to the other side, then reached out to reclaim baby Lewis. Next, came Mrs. Wade as she held onto young Harry while the two followed close behind. Keeping the promise to be as gentle as possible, two men carried Jennie's body through the same passage. Her body had been carefully wrapped into a quilt that Georgia had made in the year that Jennie turned five years old.

Once the family members had arrived safely in the cellar, Jennie's corpse was placed onto a wooden bench that was used to store milk pails and crock pots in a place located in the back corner. Still wrapped in the quilt, Jennie's apron pocket contained a photograph of Corporal Skelly, a purse, and the key to the Wade home on Breckenridge Street, all unknown at the time to Mary Wade and Georgia.

After a while, later that morning, and encouraged by several hungry soldiers, Mary Wade returned with them to the kitchen. Amid the bloodstains on the floor that remained after a quick cleansing, while not looking in that direction, Jennie's mother baked the fifteen loaves of bread and the biscuits that her loving daughter had prepared for the soldiers. It was the least she felt she could do since knowing that Jennie would not have wanted the dough to be spoiled or go to waste. In a simple way, this action would serve as a means for Mary Wade to honor the memory of the daughter which she had lost so tragically that morning.

Jennie Wade's lifeless body would lie in state

in the dimly lit cellar from eight thirty on that Friday morning, 3 July, until one o'clock in the afternoon on the following day. For nearly eighteen hours, Mary Wade and Georgia kept their mourning vigil in the cellar until they felt safe enough to come out of their dreary hiding place.

Elsewhere in Gettysburg, the townspeople were having to cope with ordeals they had never experienced before in their lifetime. Hardly a family was left untouched by the harsh effects of the war that had taken over their town. By early afternoon, an artillery duel of approximately 230 cannons began while the constant noise and vibrations were heard and felt as if the entire town was being destroyed at that very moment. This newest event continued for nearly two hours while the thunderous volleys felt like they would never cease. Then, as the guns and cannons fell silent, the Confederates massed approximately 12,000 men to strike against the left center of the Army of the Potomac, located on Cemetery Ridge and Cemetery Hill. For a time, this engagement matched both sides in a dynamic duel for supremacy, but did little to take the Union defensive position.

The thundering roar could be heard twenty towns away, while the sky above filled with giant plumes of grey smoke as the streaking fused shells were launched and dropped. Cannons boomed on top of each other by the hundreds. Human limbs cart-wheeled across the land, horses flew, ammunition wagons blew, large rocks shattered, and the hissing projectiles shrieked and exploded. Infantrymen lay with their arms-covered heads to try to drown out the deafening air and ground bursts scattered all around that was driving them mad.

Union General Hays, seen riding among his cowering riflemen, yells out words of encouragement to the troops. His men respond to him while they gather up abandoned long rifles, clean, load, and set their sights while positioning themselves along the low stone wall where the charge is expected to come.

Gibbons Division finds itself in hell while beginning to take on devastating fire power from the Federal forces nearby. Fallen horses on their backs kick and expire, human entrails drape from a fence rail, faces, bones, and torsos in red lay on the ground as splinters among the smoke filled carnage while the sun-drenched stench begins to fill the air. For all the death and havoc aimed at the Union forces, the Rebel cannon attack is not effective. Their spent ammunition could have later been used to help cover their upcoming charge.

General Meade suspects that Lee is planning to strike his center, but he is also preparing for other possibilities. He orders Robinson's Division to move up in case the Confederates try another attack on Cemetery Hill. General Lee is at his headquarters. Midway through the great cannon fire, Porter Alexander sends a message to Pickett: "If you are to advance at all, you must come at once!" The Union fire power has not let up, and Alexander already knows his artillery rounds are rapidly dwindling away. He desperately wants to have enough ammunition for his men in gray who will be soon marching out over the gentle rise of the open field. Where is Pickett? "For God's sake, come on quick or we cannot support you. Our ammo is nearly out!" Alexander scribbles out a last message to Pickett.

In an attempt to recapture the success of the previous day, the Confederates made their advance across open fields toward the Union forces in an attack that will become known as "Pickett's Charge." More than 5,000 soldiers lost their lives in one hour. By four o'clock that afternoon, following the repulse of Pickett's Charge, the Battle of Gettysburg was over, but at the time, was unknown to all the townspeople and soldiers scattered all over the town.

Throughout the evening hours, people everywhere waited fearfully while not knowing the final outcome while they huddled inside their battered houses. Rumbling sounds began to rise from Gettysburg's desolate and filthy streets by the vast movement of wagons, ambulances, and artillery pieces moving about the city. For most of the population, the worst was yet to come while they began to struggle and cope with the aftermath of war. At this time, there were twenty thousand wounded soldiers, and thousands of decomposing corpses of men, along with all the horses and mules that had been slaughtered. Sorrow and desolation cast a huge black cloud over the entire populace as the clean-up was set to begin.

An aura of deep sorrow and sadness surrounded the little brick house on Baltimore Street the next morning. The grieving Wade family now faced their own single casualty while they dealt with the loss of their beloved, Mary Virginia Wade. 4 July was Georgia's twenty-second birthday, but there would be no special celebration for her today. It had rained earlier that morning, and then once again from two until four o'clock which only added to the misery already felt by everyone who knew about the tragedy surrounding the Wade family.

An hour after the rain had finally stopped, a small gathering that consisted of Jennie's mother, her sister, her grandmother, Mrs. Elizabeth Filby, her two little brothers, Samuel and Harry, and eight soldiers, stood together in the humid seventy degree weather at the rear of the house. A muddy grave had been hastily dug in the now trampled garden in which to bury the body of Jennie Wade. Unknown at the time, but prior to the burial, Georgia had previously searched Jennie's apron pockets and removed her personal items of a tin-type of Jack, a purse, and a door key. There was no preparation for cleansing, embalming, or re-dressing her, so Jennie was merely placed into a secured oak coffin while she was still wrapped in the quilt, and lowered down into the mud-caked walls of the grave. There were no prayers, no hymns, while the family stood silently with their heads bowed as the grave diggers shoveled in the dirt clods that fell onto the casket. The body of Jennie Wade would remain in this initial grave from the afternoon of 4 July until January of the following year when her coffin would be exhumed and re-located to the cemetery which adjoined the German Reformed Church on Stratton Street.

At the time the battle was still raging, it was impossible to determine who fired the shot that actually killed Jennie Wade. Quickly, the news about the only civilian killed in Gettysburg began to circulate among soldiers, newspaper reporters, neighbors, friends, and even some townspeople who claimed that they knew the young woman. Soon after her death, there were the many concerned and curious people who came to study the angle of the bullet holes in the two doors, and the rise of three and a half inches between them. The most common and accepted conclusion about the matter came from a group of men with their inquisitive minds, intellect, and higher education. They studied each dimension by standing in the doorway and lining up the proposed angle of the shot in order to reach their final conclusion. They concluded that the fatal shot must have come from the west side of Baltimore Street, somewhere near the intersection of Emmitsburg Road, in all probability from a building at the John Rupp Tannery. There was evidence that several Louisiana Infantry companies were positioned in the southern part of town and located on both sides of Baltimore Street. Also, many of the nearby houses in the area had sustained considerable damage by the pelting of rifle fire. The homes of John M. Blocher, Harvey D. Sweney, Samuel McCreary, John Rupp, and several others had suffered extensive damages to the houses and properties. The known existence of the Union sharpshooters located in the same direction and those in direct line with the McClellan house, would help yield its final conclusion. The fatal shot that killed Jennie Wade came from the John Rupp Tannery, possibly fired by a Louisiana rifleman.

An Affair to Remember

John Wesley Culp was not the last known visitor of Jack Skelly when he was in the Taylor House Hospital in Virginia. A gentleman named John Warner from the 87th Pennsylvania Infantry visited Jack on Saturday, 11 July. During that time, Warner found him to be badly wounded and delirious at the time of his visit. Jack failed to recognize his friend who was told by the surgeon that Skelly didn't have much longer to live.

John Warner went on to report that when he saw Jack later that day, he did not seem to be suffering in any way, but just lying there on the bed in a bit of a stupor. He also mentioned that several of the men, including himself, knew that he corresponded with a young lady named

Jennie, but did not know anything about a possible engagement or plans for a wedding. It had been the sudden news about Jack's ordeal from Wes Culp that recently had been brought to Warner's attention during a time when they met, or else he would have most likely never known about him. Wes Culp was the only person who actually knew about Jack's severe wounds, and if he carried any special messages to be given either to Mrs. Skelly or Jennie Wade. At the last time Wes saw Jack in person, the two were able to talk and Wes Culp knew about his friend's terminal condition.

Johnston Hastings Skelly, Jr. died the next day, 12 July, only nine days after Wes Culp and Jennie's untimely deaths. It was said, perhaps great mercy was shown in this tragedy that these three young friends were completely unaware of each other's fate. The note, letter, or verbal message given to Wesley Culp by Jack Skelly was never delivered. Since they both died just a few days apart, there was no way to determine what Jack wanted his mother to know, or what message he wanted his mother to pass on to Jennie Wade. In the end, Wesley Culp was buried in an unmarked grave somewhere on Culp's Hill, while Jack Skelly was laid to rest in the Lutheran Cemetery in Winchester, Virginia.

On the evening of 3 July, B.S. Pendleton, an orderly with the Stonewall Brigade, met with Wes Culp's sisters, Annie and Julia, to deliver the sad news of his death. He informed them that their brother had been buried under a crooked tree on Culp's Hill, and that his grave had been plainly marked. Later, as Annie and Julia with other family members went to look for the grave site, they told everyone they were unable to locate it; however, they did find the stock of a rifle with the words *W. Culp* carved on it.

In reality, the Culp family may have found his body, and secretly decided to leave it buried there to avoid any possible anger from those in the community. After all, Wesley Culp fought for the Confederacy. Culp's grave, like so many others, was simply lost through the ravages of time and the disintegrating elements. It was generally known that most of the deceased Confederates who were buried by Union soldiers marked only a few, if any, of enemy grave sites.

Reflecting back to the events surrounding Gettysburg during the three day battle that took place there, history records that the only civilian death that occurred was only that of Miss Jennie Wade. However, there were several other civilian losses both during and after the Battle of Gettysburg.

On 1 July, the fatal shooting of an unarmed chaplain with the 90th Pennsylvania Infantry occurred on Chambersburg Street. Chaplain Horatio S. Howell was standing on the steps of the Christ Lutheran Church when he was shot and killed by a Rebel soldier.

On 3 July, a Parrot shell exploded in William Patterson's barn on the Tanneytown Road. The blast tore off the arm of a fourteen year old black boy that day around one o'clock. Also, a black man named James Godman in the Southern army was shot and killed that afternoon.

On 4 July, three men were wounded in the

town by either stray bullets or Confederates who assumed they were enemies. Jacob Gilbert was struck in the upper left arm while walking on Middle Street. Mr. Lehman, affiliated with Pennsylvania College, was wounded in the leg. Amos M. Whetstone, a seminary student who boarded with Mrs. Nancy Weikert on Chambersburg Street, was shot in the thigh by a sharpshooter.

There were also two civilians who were wounded while they joined respective military units as volunteers. John Burns, 71, was wounded in the upper thigh, the leg, and left arm, but his wounds were not considered to be serious. J.W. Weakley, age 15, was wounded in the arm and thigh while enlisted briefly with the 12th Massachusetts Infantry.

The following were a few of the civilian casualties which occurred after the battle, and not a direct result of the fighting.

On 7 July, Edward Woods, son of Alexander Woods, was shot by accident by his brother while playing with a gun he found on the battlefield.

An un-named school mate of Albertus McCreary found a shell and struck it upon a rock, causing the spark to explode while inflicting severe injuries to the boy. He was taken to a surgeon where he was pronounced dead only one hour later.

Charles M. McCurdy had two friends that were killed when they tried to open an unexploded artillery shell.

Michael Crilly was trying to unload a shell when it exploded and seriously injured his hand that required the amputation of three fingers.

Several young boys, around the age of fifteen, were playing with a gun found on the battlefield when it discharged and killed a little seven year old black girl.

Adam Taney Jr. attempted to open a shell he found in a field. The shell exploded while some of the fragments struck him in the feet and crippled him for the rest of his life.

These were but a few of the incidents that happened later in the week that so many families were left to deal with at the time. The long, hot summer days following the battle were often chaotic, turbulent, and sometimes, un-nerving, but so it went for the citizens of Gettysburg and Adams County, Pennsylvania.

Following the pathetic burial of her daughter, Mary Wade took her two sons, Samuel and Harry, and returned to her home on Breckenridge Street on the evening of 5 July. This left Georgia alone to care for her infant, and along with Catharine McClain, both women were faced with bringing restored order to the respective sides of their house. Mary Wade walked into her house expecting the worse, but it appeared to be in much better shape than her daughter Georgia's battered home. It had been ransacked, with minor interior damages, but a lot of sweeping, cleaning, and straightening misplaced items and furniture would yield an acceptable new beginning. At least, there had been no fire to destroy the existing structure. Samuel and Harry both pitched in to help their mother who hadn't even had the time as yet to grieve.

During the last few days of July, almost three weeks after the death of her sister, Georgia

McClellan made a sudden change in her life. After leaving the baby in the care of her mother, Georgia went to serve as a nurse to the sick and wounded soldiers in the Adams County Court House in Gettysburg, which was being used as a hospital. She only worked there for one week when she was transferred to the United States Army General Hospital at Wolf's Grove. Also known as Camp Letterman, the hospital was located two miles east of Gettysburg. Georgia worked for the next two years at various times in other medical facilities while lending her services to the ill and wounded soldiers during the time her husband was away serving in the army. Her mother remained in Gettysburg where she continued to take care of Lewis, who kept her extremely busy, along with doing occasional alterations as needed for her regular customers. Mrs. Wade was surprised shortly after the battle to receive a letter from President Lincoln expressing both praise and condolences in the death of Jennie for service to her country. When the President later visited Gettysburg on 18-19 November 1863, to dedicate the Soldier's National Cemetery, he requested that Georgia McClellan sit with him on the platform, along with all the other invited dignitaries. Georgia told her mother that she didn't want to attend, let alone to be seated on the speaker's platform, but Mary Wade insisted that she should go to represent the Wade family, but mainly because President Lincoln had invited her. Georgia was always indifferent to lots of pomp and circumstance, long boring speeches, and herself, being in the public eye to have people she didn't even know to scrutinize her for whatever reason.

Georgia's husband, John Louis McClellan, survived the war years and later returned home to Gettysburg. In 1867, the McClellan family moved to Denison, Iowa to be close to their dear friends, the Laub family, who had moved west from Pennsylvania a few years earlier. Georgia and Louis had five children: Lewis Kenneth, Virginia Wade, James Britton, Nellie Georgia, and John Harry McClellan. Georgia Wade McClellan died in Carroll, Iowa on 7

September 1927 at age eighty-six, following the death of her husband in 1913.

Like their sister, Georgia, the three brothers grew up and all moved west to live out the rest of their lives. Most likely, it was probably rather difficult to remain around the house where their sister had died so tragically.

John James Wade, also called Jack, was the brother who last saw his sister Jennie on 26 June 1863, on the day she altered his uniform when they both said their farewell to each other as he rode away. Jack survived the war, returned home for a brief time, and in 1866, he moved to Denison, Iowa. From there, he headed westward with the Union Pacific Railroad to California. Whenever a better opportunity surfaced for him, he moved once more and took up his new residence in Nevada. At some point, he met Julia Rush from Texas and they were married on 17 March 1875 in Clover Valley, Colorado. The couple made their home eventually in Mancos, Colorado for 42 years where John and Julia had five children. John James Wade died in Kayenta, Arizona in Navajo County on 2 September 1925 at age seventy-nine.

Samuel Wade was the twelve year old brother arrested for trying to save his employer's horse from the small band of Confederates. He married Elizabeth "Lizzie" Johns from York Springs, Pennsylvania on 17 November 1869 at age nineteen. He worked in Gettysburg, sometimes as a house painter, and it is unknown if he and Lizzie had any children. The couple later moved to Peoria, Illinois where Samuel Swan Wade died in 1935 at age eighty-five.

Harry Wade, the eight year old brother who witnessed his sister's death at the McClellan house, left Gettysburg at an early age and moved to Nebraska. At some point, he moved to Seattle, Washington where he met and married his wife, Mary. Harry Marion Wade died in Seattle at the age of fifty-five on 26 September 1906.

James Wade Sr., Jennie's father, died at the age of fifty-eight on 10 July 1872. He spent his last years as a sick and broken man in the Adams County Alms House. He was buried in the Evergreen Cemetery in Gettysburg on 11 July 1872.

Mary Wade probably experienced the greatest loss in the passing of her daughter, Jennie, while she stood at the stove nearby and watched her fall to the floor and die right before her eyes. How tragic, but never realizing that the one lone shot could have easily struck her instead. During the days that followed, Mary Wade found peace and solace in the blessing that Jennie had been taken quickly and unknowingly. The grieving mother not only lost a loving, caring daughter, but someone who helped support her financially while the two worked together as well-known seamstresses in their home on Breckenridge Street. Also, now there was no one to help with all the household chores and the care of Sam, Harry, and little Isaac Brinkerhoff. During the days following the battle, Mary Wade depended on help and comfort from her parents, Samuel and Elizabeth Filby, who resided in a house located close by where Jennie had been killed. Despite all the many hardships, Mary continued to live in her house on Breckenridge Street until she died at age seventy-two. Mary Ann Filby Wade was buried in the Evergreen Cemetery on 31 December 1892.

Lewis McClellan, whose birth caused Jennie and her mother to gather at the deadly McClellan house, grew up in Gettysburg. Later, he moved to Billings, Montana in 1906 where he resided for sixteen years. Lewis was married with two sons. After a two-year illness, he died in Billings on 12 February 1941. Lewis Kenneth McClellan was seventy-seven.

In November 1864, Daniel Skelly had his brother Jack returned to Gettysburg and interred in the Evergreen Cemetery.

In November 1865, the family of Mary Virginia Wade had her body exhumed once again from the cemetery at the German Reformed Church and re-interred in the Evergreen Cemetery near the burial site of Jack Skelly.

On 16 September 1901, the Jennie Wade monument was unveiled in the Evergreen

Cemetery. It is located about 100 yards from the grave of Johnson Hastings Skelly, Jr.

The inscription on the monument reads:

Jennie Wade
Killed July 3, 1863
while making bread for Union soldiers

Part 2

My Story

by Jennie Wade

I was born at home in Gettysburg, Pennsylvania on 21 May 1843, and given the name, Mary Virginia Wade. My parents were James and Mary Ann Filby Wade.

My first recollection of being alive came to me when I was almost four years old. I remember playing dolls with my sister. Mama said that I called her George, but her given name was Georgia Anna. Sometimes, my sister was mean to me, but I always loved her anyway.

Mama was pretty, always smiling, while I watched her sit in her rocking chair and sew. She made all our clothes, and I was happy when she would make me a new dress. Most of the time, I wore hand-me-downs from my sister whenever she out-grew her clothes. When I was six years old, one of my favorite dresses that

Mama made for me was the long blue velvet one that almost reached the floor.

I don't remember much about my father since he was committed to the poor house when I was almost ten years old. He was a tailor, and had a business in our house until he fell into bad health, and Mama had my father put away. She claimed that he went insane. I never saw him after that.

Beside Georgia and myself, our parents also had our three brothers, Jack, Samuel, and Harry. We all grew up in a house on Breckenridge Street. All of us were christened at Trinity Reformed Church as infants, and baptized there. Later, I was confirmed and united with the St. James Lutheran Church on York Street.

Miss Abigail Crenshaw, my primary school teacher, always called me Mary Virginia; however, my family called me "Ginnie." Sometime later, I would become known as Jennie for the rest of my life.

My best girlfriend was Maren Bathurst, who lived over on Baltimore Street with her parents, Richard and Katherine, who were originally from Kansas. Maren and I had known each other since the third grade in school, and we both liked the same boy when we were sixteen. Mr. Bathurst was a banker; however, Maren's mother no longer worked, but had been a governess to the Reynolds children when they lived in Kansas City.

Maren and I spent a lot of time together during our early teen years. We were almost inseparable while our relationship continued to grow each passing day. I always thought of Maren as being my other sister. There were many times that she would stay over at our house, and Mama would sit us both down while she taught us to sew. I would always let Maren think that she was the best seamstress, although we both knew that I could out-stitch her, even if I were to be blindfolded. However, she did have a dainty, precise little stitch when it came to sewing a piece of delicate French lace onto a dress collar or sleeve. I have to admit that was the one thing she could always do much better than I, but still not as good as Mama. My mother was the most gifted seamstress that I ever knew in all of Gettysburg.

Maren's birthday was in February before mine was in May, so when we were sixteen that year, we found ourselves in competition over the affections we both had for the new boy at school. It wasn't a contest, but simply a challenge to see if either of us could get him to like us enough to steal a kiss. The victor would attain bragging rights as to which one of us that he liked best, while his kiss would become the ultimate prize. I remember him just like it was yesterday.

Julian Hargraves sent my heart racing the first moment I saw him as he entered the classroom and took a seat on the bench in the second row. He was almost a head taller than most of the boys in class, while having a muscular build and a deeply tanned complexion. He looked so handsome with his bright blue eyes and shoulder-length coal black hair. I could tell by the new clothes he wore that he came from a well-to-do family from somewhere other than Gettysburg.

After Miss Crenshaw called him up before the class for his introduction as a new pupil, I was delighted to learn more about the seventeen year old. His full name was Julian Cavanaugh Hargraves, but he preferred to be called Jules. His parents were Dr. Fenton Hargraves and Mrs. Julia Cavanaugh Hargraves who had recently moved here from Baltimore. They lived in the old Hadley farmhouse out on the Emmitsburg Road. Dr. Hargraves was employed as a surgeon at the infirmary, while his wife stayed at home and loved gardening and doing needlepoint.

Several weeks had passed before Maren and I actually had the chance to personally talk to Jules. It was she who came up with the idea of trying to get him to kiss either of us. We all three met that year at tryouts for our school play to be performed in November. Miss Crenshaw simply loved anything written by Shakespeare, so this year's play was going to be "Romeo and Juliet." Needless to say, Jules Hargraves got the part of Romeo, while Maren beat me out to steal the role of Juliet from me. I was a bit disappointed to land the part of Lady Capulet, her mother, but at least I had a speaking part and wasn't in the ensemble cast. Soon, we were all trying to learn our lines while rehearsals began that October. After-school rehearsals went well, while Miss Crenshaw insisted that there was to be no kissing during the balcony scene. Kissing in public was considered to be in bad taste, often leading to possible scandalous affairs and idle gossip, so she was quick to emphasize her feelings while she kept reminding everyone.

The play was scheduled to be presented as a weekend event in November on Friday and Saturday nights with a matinee on Sunday afternoon. The performance on Friday was a little shaky with Maribel McKenzie forgetting several of her lines, along with a prop mix-up and a piece of scenery falling and nearly hitting Thomas Blackstone on the head. Everything went much better on Saturday night, and we received an unexpected standing ovation. Then, the matinee on Sunday came as a total shock to the audience, Miss Crenshaw, and especially to me. It was during the balcony scene when Jules, as Romeo, took Maren in his arms and kissed her right on the mouth. It wasn't a long kiss, but he definitely put his mouth onto hers. I was standing off stage, but I could clearly see the action on stage as well as Miss Crenshaw in the wings who nearly fainted against one of the props. The audience went wild as several rose to their feet while creating an outburst of shouting, cheering, jeering, and applauding until order was resumed for the play to continue.

Although it didn't happen like we had originally planned, I had to accept that Maren, under this unique guise, had gotten the first kiss from Jules; however, it wouldn't be the last. Following our graduation, almost one year later, Maren became Mrs. Julian Cavanaugh Hargraves and had a beautiful baby daughter that she named Virginia Julianne Hargraves. She would call the rosy-cheeked, black-haired, baby girl "Julie." Jules Hargraves loved his two girls so much, and while he was becoming established as a young carpenter's apprentice, he built Maren a two-story brick house on York Street where they set up housekeeping.

It was during my last two years at school

when I became close friends with my classmates, John Wesley Culp and Jack Skelly. We usually took our lunch together, and sometimes at recess we would all sit under the big chestnut tree and share our hopes and dreams for the future. Wes wanted to follow his father as a farmer on Culp's Hill or join the military as a soldier. He didn't have a steady girl, but I could tell that he liked me. Jack's father expected him to follow in his business as a tailor, but the young Mr. Skelly was interested in becoming a stone cutter, and one day to operate his own business as a successful stone mason. As for me, I wanted to fall in love, get married, and have a family.

As the affection I once felt for Jules Hargraves faded rapidly away, I suddenly became drawn to Jack Skelly. Certainly, Wes Culp would always be a dear friend, but I could feel myself wanting to be around Jack at every possible opportunity. How I longed for him to take notice of me, and ask my mother if he could possibly begin to see me, other than at school. Did I love him? At eighteen, I thought surely I must. I certainly didn't dislike him.

Jack was so good looking with his long brown hair and blue eyes. He was always smiling and grinning, especially during the times when he would try to grow a beard or moustache. We both laughed about that before his facial hair began to grow more thickly on his handsome face. Jack told me that he would always remember me as Lady Capulet, but he thought I should have gotten the part of Juliet instead of Maren. I took that comment as one of the nicest complements that he ever told me. I felt that I had his interest, now I just had to provide him with a little more encouragement. After all, he was extremely quiet and shy, especially when there were just the two of us alone on rare occasions. I wanted more attention than just the few times that Jack would show up for a church service, and ask to sit with me on Sunday morning.

I was completely surprised on the last day of school that year when Jack asked me to go to the school picnic with him. Each year, during the first week in June, the ending of the school year was celebrated with a picnic held on the school grounds. This annual event honored those students who had recently graduated, along with those who would return in the Fall for their last year of school. The participating families would provide a covered dish, meet at the school for the picnic lunch, and later that evening, were invited to attend a dance at the Wagon Hotel operated by Conrad and Catherine Snyder.

On the day of the picnic, as I remember, I had spent all morning trying my best to get ready. I tried on three of my favorite dresses, decided on the one I would wear, and put the iron into the fire to heat. Later, while ironing the dress, I burned two fingers and nearly scorched a small place on the back of the bodice. I suddenly found myself moving entirely too fast and I needed to slow down. This very afternoon would be my first date with Jack, and I was filled with joy and excitement. I needed to look my best, and now my hair was plastered to my head with long strands hanging down my back like barbed wire. At last, all I could do was brush it all out, braid it, and put it up underneath a pretty white lace cap that belonged to my sister, Georgia. When I finally put on my favorite linen dress, dyed to a beautiful shade of crimson, my heel caught the bottom and ripped the seam. As I bent down to pull the skirt up to re-stitch the hemline, a pearl button popped off the back and hit the floor. I was almost in tears when Georgia came in, bringing words of encouragement, while she helped me finish getting ready for my first date. She even let me wear her cameo pendant while she tied the black velvet ribbon around my neck. Now, I was ready at last, taking my final glance into the looking glass while I waited for Jack Skelly to arrive.

A loud knock brought my little brother Harry to his feet while he ran to open the front door. Standing there on the porch was Jack, right on time, sporting a fresh haircut and having a big grin on his face. From where I was seated, he looked so dashing in what I suspected was a new pair of black leather boots. He was dressed in a pair of black gabardine trousers and a pale blue cotton shirt without a collar and the top button unfastened. I rose to my feet and hurried across the room to greet him at the door. I invited him inside for a brief wait while Mama finished packing her fried chicken into a basket and covering it with a fresh linen towel. Jack offered to carry the basket for her while we made ready to leave the house and walk to the schoolyard.

Jack was the true gentleman while he escorted us to the picnic as we laughed and talked all the way to the school. He always seemed to be in a good mood without a care in the world. There were many times in my life that I wished I could do the same.

Mama took her basket from Jack while she and Harry started toward the food table where Miss Crenshaw stood to receive all the food items. Jack pulled me aside, took my arm, and asked if I would walk with him down by the creek before we had our lunch. He had something that he wanted to ask in private. I couldn't imagine what it could be, so I smiled at him and gave him a simple nod of agreement. He held onto my hand while we strolled along the creek bank.

I was rather shocked and surprised at the mere mention of the name, Jules Hargraves. Jack asked me if I was in love with Jules. I had to admit that I was drawn to him on the first day I saw him. I wanted him to like me, so I went on to confess to Jack all about the scheme Maren and I made up together in order to get Jules to kiss one of us. Maren was my dearest friend, and when she won his heart, Jules became a friend as well. So, the three of us were always just good friends. Jack seemed to be relieved while hearing this news. He escorted me back to the gathering crowd where we enjoyed the picnic together.

From an early age, Mama had raised Georgia and I to become a respected lady, polished, poised, and refined with unquestionable conduct at all times. Her rules of proper etiquette were not to be taken lightly; she was rather a strict enforcer, especially when it came to eating and dining in public. A lady always took small dainty bites, chewed slowly with her mouth closed, and never talked with food in her mouth. In her own words, she emphasized that we should eat like a bird and not like a common field hand or vagabond. I try to remember all she taught us, while I'm feasting on a plate of boiled corn, lima beans, carrots, potatoes, and a chicken leg with a slice of apple pie for dessert.

On the day of the picnic, my brother John Wade, who we all called Jack, was at work. My brother, Samuel, remained at home with my sister, Georgia, to help take care of Isaac Brinkerhoff, the little crippled boy we kept while his mother worked in town. Mama, Harry, Jack Skelly, and I had almost finished our lunch when Jo Anna Duchesne (*doo-shane*) and her son, Billy, took a seat at a table by themselves. Everyone who was seated nearby, stopped eating or talking long enough to glance quickly at them and then resume back to normal as if they could care less. I felt it was a shame the way most people treated Mrs. Duchesne, and especially Billy. Poor Billy!

He was known at school as "Melon-head,"

while some of the older boys would often call him that to his face. Billy was a year older than I, and he looked forward to finishing school next year. He was a slow reader, but good at arithmetic and anything to do with numbers. Mrs. Duchesne provided their only means of support while they both lived together in a rented house on York Street. She worked long hours as a clerk at Crawford Mercantile. Most everyone in the school and their neighborhood knew all about the Duchesne family.

John Duchesne had been a successful attorney during the time he lived in Vanderburgh County, Indiana. His law office was located on the square in Evansville where he partnered at Baker, Billings, Copeland, and Duchesne. At age forty-five, the single, dark-haired lawyer was on his way to becoming the district attorney when he met an attractive young brunette named Jo Anna Lawson, whom Mr. Baker had hired as a legal secretary for their law firm. Miss Lawson was thirty-six, pretty, and also single. It wasn't long until John Duchesne fell in love with Jo Anna, and he married her when she became six months pregnant. He built her a fashionable four bedroom house, located in the downtown district on Abercrombie Street, and allowed her to furnish it as she saw fit. The most remarkable feature of the townhouse was the elaborate spiral staircase that descended onto the white marble floor in the foyer. It was on this staircase that the accident involving Jo Anna occurred when she was just a few weeks away from delivery.

That particular evening, John Duchesne came home late after he left Fanelli's Tavern, and continued his drinking there for the rest of the night. Jo Anna had locked herself into the upstairs bedroom after a very heated argument with her drunken husband. Around midnight, he staggered upstairs and began pounding on her bedroom door until she finally gave in and opened the door. She attempted to rush past him while trying to make it to the top of the stairs, but she couldn't move very fast on account of her present condition. Suddenly, he grabbed her arms and pinned her against the top railing. More harsh words were spoken in anger while Jo Anna pulled away while trying to free herself from his hold. John continued to shout his hurtful curse words at her while they struggled at the top of the stairs. As Jo Anna broke free from him, she fell backward and landed three steps down while her protruding mid-section crashed solidly against the railing. The fall broke out three of the wooden spindles on the bannister, while it was said later to be a miracle that the short fall had saved her life. A tumble down the entire staircase would have most certainly meant instant death for her and her unborn baby.

The doctor and sheriff were immediately summoned to the Duchesne home where Jo Anna was examined, sedated, and put to bed for the remainder of her pregnancy. It was truly a relief and miracle that she did not lose the baby. Also, at the same time of the accident, the sheriff arrived on the scene to take a statement from her husband, survey the situation, and file a written report. After a rather lengthy interrogation by the sheriff, he ruled that the fall taken by Mrs. Duchesne was to be listed as an unfortunate accident. John Duchesne never really escaped the scrutiny of his involvement concerning the accident as lingering questions continued to surface over the next few years. Was Jo Anna's fall really an accident? Did she stumble and fall by herself or did John Duchesne simply push her?

Two weeks later, the six pound baby boy that Jo Anna named Billy, was born at home. He appeared to be a strong, healthy infant, but with one unfortunate condition which affected the right side of his elongated face and head. The doctor concluded that as a result of Jo Anna's accident, the fall against the railing had pressed upon the baby's head hard enough to cause the distinct deformity in the skull. In the months following, Billy's head grew slightly larger than normal while the right side of his face began to sink in and his right eye began to bulge as it caused his facial features to appear as most people would call hideous. By the time Billy was a year old, his head appeared to be growing much too large for his body while the right side of his face continued to pull inward.

For whatever reason, known only to them, John divorced Jo Anna that year while she took her son and moved to Gettysburg to be close to her sister, Janelle Lawson-Davies. I really didn't know Billy's mother all that well, but he was a remarkable young man who was a fellow classmate at school. He was really smart and could play a banjo the best I ever heard. I agreed with Mama when she always said that we should look at a person from the inside, and not the outward appearance. Billy was my special friend, and all he needed was lots of love, not pity. He told me that after he finished school, he wanted to go to California and see the Pacific Ocean, maybe even take a swim in it. I remember asking him last year if he ever got to see his father, and he said that he had only seen a photograph of him taken several years ago. His father had made it quite clear that he never wanted to see Billy again.

John Duchesne continued his life as a successful district attorney in Vanderburgh County, where he lived for the next twelve years with his wife, Emma Lee, and three children, two girls and a boy. It was doubtful that Emma Lee and the children ever knew anything about Jo Anna and Billy. At age fifty-seven, John Elliot Duchesne was found murdered in the back alley of Fanelli's Tavern with his throat slit from ear to ear, and his body dumped onto a pile of garbage. He had been robbed of ten dollars in silver and his gold-plated pocket watch and chain. His unknown assailant was never captured, and the murder remained unsolved in the cold case file in the sheriff's office.

After we all finished our lunch, I stopped briefly to say a word to Mrs. Duchesne and Billy before Jack walked us back home. I needed to rest for a while before he would return and take me to the dance later that evening. Also, I needed to change into a more formal gown and the shoes that were more suitable for dancing. I couldn't hardly wait until tonight to get Jack Skelly out on the dance floor.

The Wagon Hotel was lit up by nightfall, while the soft glow of the flickering candle light on the tables and the gaslights suspended from the ceiling filled the ballroom with all its beauty of illumination while the guests began to arrive. Mr. and Mrs. Snyder, the proprietors, stood in the doorway while they ushered Jack and I into the lobby, and directed us across the spacious room toward the ballroom where the dance was set to begin promptly by eight.

Conrad and Catherine Snyder had owned the Wagon Hotel since 1859 after the passing of his father from the typhoid. Their family was originally from Philadelphia, but following the death of his aging father, the adventurous Mister Conrad decided to move to Gettysburg and spend his inheritance by purchasing and operating the newly constructed hotel. Along with his young bride, Catherine, the couple soon began to enjoy the success of their new business venture. The hotel was built relatively close to the Emmitsburg Road, one of the more traveled wagon routes in and out of town, so the name of the Wagon Hotel suited the opulent structure almost perfectly.

Several of my classmates had already arrived for the dance, while the first person I saw was our friend, Wesley Culp. He was seated alone at a table and sipping on a cup of apple cider as we made our approach. After we greeted him, Jack excused himself momentarily, while he left the ballroom. Wes invited me to have a seat next to him while he began to engage me in pleasant conversation. In the next few minutes, Wes Culp shared with me many things about himself that I never knew.

Having been born in Gettysburg in 1839, John Wesley Culp was almost four years older than me. He had already finished school last year, and was presently working at Mr. William Hoffman's carriage shop where he did upholstery work on the more stylish rigs that the shop newly built, repaired, or sold as is. I thought he was exceptionally gifted at his work, especially by creating the fancy leather-tufted seat covers that he handcrafted on site.

Wes Culp was a short, little man who stood no more than five feet tall, even when wearing his high-heeled boots. He kept his sandy-colored hair cut to shoulder length, and usually had a bushy beard and moustache. He had dark brown eyes and a smile that made me break out with a grin each time I saw him. I asked him what he was doing alone at the dance, and he told me that Miss Crenshaw had invited him. He suspected that she was planning to set him up with the readily available Miss Maribel McKenzie. He confessed to me that was never happening, and then surprised me with his latest plan. He was going to enlist in the infantry, but not only that, it was going to be with the Confederate army.

I had to ask him why he would even consider such a thing, knowing that his brother William had already enlisted as a corporal in Company E of the Second Pennsylvania Volunteers. What would Will and the rest of his family have to say about this when they found out? Rumors of war had already surfaced while the talk kept mounting about the southern troops headed toward Pennsylvania. Why then, for Heaven's sakes, the Confederate forces? He just sat there as though he never heard me ask the question, then looked at me in a state of seriousness and gave me his reply. He told me that Mr. Hoffman was moving his shop and business to Shepherdstown, Virginia, and that he, Thaddeus Markle, Fredrick Cooper, and his little brother Charley, were joining him there to work. Thad Markle heard from a relative in Virginia that if he or any of his friends were to enlist in the Confederate army, they each could obtain a sizeable bonus for joining. The only downside would be if their unit were called to active duty, then they would have to leave their jobs and join in the fight.

By this time, Jack was back at the table where we sat and talked a while about our old school days until the stringed quartet broke out the music to the next quadrille. Jack always preferred the more popular waltz, but I loved dancing in a lively quadrille whenever I had the chance to do so. We excused ourselves from the company of Wes Culp, and took to the dance floor to form our place with the other three couples who had motioned for us to join them. Jack had only danced in a quadrille on one other occasion, while he had to ask me again how to do it. By the time I finished my brief explanation, he knew the complete history of the dance.

The quadrille was first introduced in France around 1760, possibly at the palace of Versailles. Later on, its popularity soon spread throughout Europe, as well as the American colonies. The dance was a form of cotillion in which four couples began by forming the sides of a square. The couples in each corner of the square took turns in performing the dance, where one couple would dance while the others rested until their turn. One pair was called the "head" couple, while the adjacent pairs, the "side" couples. The dance was first started and performed by the head couple, and then repeated by the sides. It was a fun, fast-moving dance which kept a gentleman's feet in a precise, perpetual motion while the lady's flowing skirts swirled around the floor as they turned. The terms called out in the dance were mostly the same as those mentioned in ballet, such as *jete'*, *chasse'*, *croise'*, *plie'*, and *arabesque*.

Following the third quadrille, Jack was ready to take me home. How I loved dancing with that man and being with him as often as I could. It wasn't long after the dance until Mama began to depend on me to help her with her sewing since her business had taken on several new customers. I agreed to help out, what else could I do?

During this time, we took in little Isaac Brinkerhoff, a six year old crippled boy. His mother was a regular customer of Mama's, and Mrs. Brinkerhoff needed a caretaker during the hours she worked across town. Most of the time, Isaac ended up living with us for days at a time. He wasn't much trouble since he had mastered the use of his crutches and could get around the house with a certain ease. His misfortune came on the day he was playing in the street, and got trampled by a runaway wild stallion who had broken away from his owner, Mr. Lewis Danielson. The final operation that had to be done on his legs left him with his eventual crippled condition. He was always in good spirits, and seemed to enjoy playing with me a game of "hide the thimble" and the guessing game of "I Spy". I was the only one he would let cut his hair whenever it was time for that to happen.

In the winter of 1861-62, the civil war was now in its seventh month, while news of its impending battles brought forth somewhat distressing news to the residents of Gettysburg. The 10th New York Calvary Regiment, known as the "Porter Guards", were ordered to Gettysburg to be stationed here for three months to protect the state borders from any threat or intrusion by the Confederate forces. The New Yorkers spent their long wintry days by drilling and perfecting their use of sabers and small arms on a regular basis each day. It was during that time when Mama, Georgia, and I became acquainted with several of the soldiers who brought us their uniforms when they needed repair. I'll never forget the day I met Corporal Heath Callahan from New York.

I was alone in the shop early on that particular morning, while having the task of the re-arrangement of several heavy bolts of material when I heard a light rap at the door. The door swung back to reveal a very handsome young corporal, and what appeared to be two of his friends. The corporal seemed to be a bit nervous and excited while he entered the room and introduced himself as Corporal Heath Callahan and his two friends, Lt. Jake Lancaster and Pvt. Harry Burkhalter. I must admit that the tall young man immediately caught my attention with his sandy blond hair, blue eyes, and boyish grin with a dimple in his chin. But, alas, his good looks failed in comparison to my own Jack Skelly. I noticed that he kept his hands concealed and positioned firmly around his backside as he stood before me while he shifted his feet back and forth very nervously.

It was then that he revealed his embarrassing predicament to me while he turned around, dropped his hands, and bent slightly forward to show me his rosy pink cheeks. Hoping to put him at ease, I mentioned that I had two younger brothers, and seeing a young boy's behind wasn't anything that I hadn't seen before, nor was I offended by seeing his own perfectly rounded buttocks. Of course, I didn't admit to him how this sight made my heart start to flutter. He apologized for not wearing his drawers on this day since he was in a rush to get dressed and make it on time to his drill. I tried my best to keep a straight face and not laugh aloud while I assured him that I could stitch those pants in just a few minutes.

The corporal commenced to tell me how he had ripped out the back seat of his pants and now had less than a half hour to present himself fully-dressed and ready for his morning drill. He continued by saying there was not enough time to return to his camp site to change his uniform. I had him step behind the dressing screen and remove his split trousers while he quickly followed my instructions. Within ten minutes, I had his blue woolen uniform pants stitched up and ready to wear. Corporal Callahan seemed very grateful and pleased while he thanked me, and told me that I had saved him from receiving a demerit for improper dress. When I told him that there was no charge for my simple service, he insisted that I take one dollar for the materials, and so, I did. I continued to see the young corporal and some of the Porter Guards for the next three months until their regiment was removed from Gettysburg. I still think about Corporal Heath Callahan from time to time, although I will probably never know whatever happened to him while the war continued to head our way. I pray the good Lord will keep watch over him and his friends, and return them safely home to their families after this terrible war comes to an end.

Now, I am thinking about my own true love, Jack Skelly, and our last night together. He had enlisted with the 8th Corps Infantry weeks ago, and his unit was leaving early in the morning for Virginia. We hurriedly hatched a plan to meet in the gazebo at St. James Lutheran Church that particular night. After my chores were all done, I told Mama that I was walking to Georgia's house to spend the night with her. Neither she, nor my sister, knew of my plan to meet Jack that night to say our goodbyes. It was a still and quiet night while the late evening darkening gave way to the moon and stars as their twinkling beams filled the sky, thus providing me a perfect light while I made my walk to the gazebo. There he was, waiting patiently for me to arrive.

We kissed and embraced while I fell into his waiting arms. He led me to a bench where we sat while I held onto his warm hand as he put his other arm around my shoulder and drew me close. We kissed once again, and then Jack turned to look me directly in the face while we began to voice our inmost feelings toward each other. After what seemed like a short time, almost an hour had passed, and he regretfully told me that he must leave to finish packing. He would be gone by the time of the next sunrise.

I was willing to fully give myself to him that very moment, but he drew back and told me that now we must wait. So, we both promised to wait until he returned, and then we would marry and spend the rest of our lives together. If anything should happen to him, he told me that I should find happiness with someone else, but know that he will always love me no matter what may come. He didn't intend to make me a widow, so we must wait for now, and marry when he returned home. My tears began to fall while I pulled my shawl close around me to catch them. Jack pulled me close, and kissed me for the last time. After he felt that I had composed myself somewhat, he stood, turned, and walked away into the dark of night while never looking back. I watched him leave until I could no longer see him. I lingered in the gazebo for a while, then left to spend a sleepless night at Georgia's. I placed his photograph on my bedside table, and kept staring at it for the rest of the night until the candle finally went out. I never spoke a word about this meeting to Mama or Georgia, but somehow I felt that my sister always knew.

As I recall, on 26 June 1863, I was home alone with Isaac and Harry. I had just finished hemming a dress for Mrs. Rosemary Watkins when a strange feeling suddenly came over me. It had only been six days since an important telegram had been received by the people of Gettysburg. The message from Governor Andrew W. Curtin stated that all residents should begin to move their stores and possessions to a more secure location and seek their own protection. The news suddenly frightened a number of civilians who found themselves with no place to go and near panic to the elderly and those physically infirmed. The townspeople could only hope and pray that all the rumors going around would prove to be untrue, but that was not meant to be. Suddenly, as a thief in the night, came our worst fear – *Invasion*.

I soon learned that Confederate General Jubal A. Early's men had been spotted over on Chambersburg Street as the news spread while several men were yelling just outside my door. They shouted that officers were seen waving their swords while the troops were firing their weapons into the air. I gathered Harry and Isaac, and went to a window to look outside. People were running everywhere, and now I heard the gunfire as it echoed down the street and all over town. I tried to remain calm as not to upset the boys.

On that particular Friday afternoon, Mama was staying with my sister at her house on Baltimore Street where Georgia had just given birth to her baby about one hour prior to the invasion by the Confederacy. This news came to me in a note from Mama only a half hour before the occupation. It was delivered by Lil' Roscoe, one of Tillie Johnson's seven children. Georgia's husband, Louis McClellan, was presently away and serving with the Northern army in Virginia, so it fell to Mama to be there with my sister. All I knew was that Georgia had a healthy baby boy. Now, I had so many other things to think about rather than birthing babies. My heart was racing, and I knew that all my strength, courage, and faith was about to be tested.

Earlier that morning, before there were any thoughts about an impending invasion, this twenty year old girl was about to become a woman while taking over brand new and challenging responsibilities. I was rapidly assuming several jobs that would have belonged to my late father while I vaguely remember him as a ten year old.

My brother John, whom we all call Jack, needed my help with his uniform. Now, at age seventeen, he had enlisted in Company B of the 21st Pennsylvania Calvary only three days ago, and had been given his assignment as a bugler. Jack was short for his age, and only stood five feet three inches tall. The uniform he was issued was almost two sizes too big, so I had to complete all the necessary alterations in haste. Jack's regiment had been ordered that very morning to leave for scouting duty in southern Pennsylvania by way of the York Road. This was all happening only a few hours before the Confederates were expected to arrive from the opposite direction. We both hurriedly packed his gear onto his horse and said our fond goodbyes. I watched him ride out alone into the unknown where he would try to catch up with his company which had already departed. He turned to give me a wave, and as the dust rose up from the road, he was gone. Somehow, I felt that I would never see him again.

My brother, Samuel, age twelve, lived and worked as a delivery boy for James Pierce who was a butcher in his shop at the end of Breckenridge Street. I could only pray that he would remain safe and out of harm's way. What is going to happen to all of us?

The next morning, General Jubal A. Early's Division left Gettysburg while we all felt a sigh of relief. This overnight occupation certainly made us all feel now what we were up against, and what we could expect to come in the days ahead. I had never experienced anything like this in my life so far, so naturally I was a bit scared and worried, as many of our local residents. While fear and alarm continued to rise, I discovered that many of the able-bodied citizens began to find ways to secure and protect their property and themselves from the threats of the Confederate invaders. There wasn't much that could be done to hide or shield the animals that were scattered all over the town; however, some of the horses were taken into the woods or down by the river to hide since they were more easily to move. I heard Mr. Pierce tell a group of men that the horses would be considered a prized bounty if they fell into the hands of the enemy.

On Monday, 29 June, it was reported that

nearly 13,000 Confederate troops were camped on the outskirts of town. By nightfall, I could see their campfires spread along the eastern slope of the mountain, only nine miles to the west.

By early evening the next day, 30 June, the first Northern soldiers appeared in Gettysburg in search of Lee's army that was positioned nearby. Following a long and tiring ride, they arrived along the southern route in the vicinity of the Emmitsburg Road. My brother, Samuel, told me later how the Federal Calvary men were heartily welcomed by the many loyal citizens who stood to applaud and cheer them while they made their entrance. After positioning pickets in the north and west of town, the horse soldiers were dispersed among the farms of James McPherson, James J. Wills, and John Forney. By nightfall, the armies were in place while they were waiting on their orders. While the darkness of the night drew its curtain across the sky, we settled down for our last night of peaceful sleep. I went to bed with thoughts of what tomorrow might bring.

By eight o'clock the next morning on 1 July, it seemed to me that all hell had broken loose. Shells from the western battery awoke us all with the sound of exploding noises both near and in the town. I opened the front door to look out, and as I stood on the porch, I saw several neighbors as they gathered outside their houses in panic as they shouted at each other while starting to flee down the street.

Clayton Messer called out to me as he passed by the house. He shared the news that General Heth's Division of the Confederacy were advancing toward town. This unit consisted of nearly 6,000 infantrymen who were rapidly approaching from the west. As the conflict began, I could hear the shelling from the western battery. The flying projectiles would soon send us scrambling down into our basements or leaving our homes to seek other places of refuge. I had to make a quick decision about what I needed to do.

I decided to gather a few things and take Harry and Isaac immediately over to Georgia's house. My little brother didn't want to go, but

I knew that I would feel better to be with my mother and sister. When we were ready to leave, I locked the front door while I doubted whether the war would permit me to ever return home again. Harry asked me why I took the time to lock up the house. If the soldiers wanted in, a locked door wouldn't stop them.

Mama met me at the door when we arrived at Georgia's. I was immediately met with the task of helping her with all the household chores. I found Georgia and the baby seated on a chaise in the parlor, and I gave her a hug while she let me hold her newborn son, Lewis Kenneth McClellan. He was a fine looking boy with good color and bright blue eyes.

So many things needed my utmost attention: Isaac needed to use the chamber pot; Harry wanted to venture outside in the yard to see all the soldiers posted along the street; the baby kept crying and needed changing; Georgia wanted a cup of hot tea; and Mama, in preparation of the next meal, needed me to wash up all the dirty dishes. In the meantime, there was a pounding at the door. I opened it to reveal a lone, young soldier in a dirty blue uniform begging for a cup of water. I poured him a dipper of water into a tin cup and offered him a cold stale biscuit leftover from breakfast which he quickly took from my hand. He looked as if he were surprised to see me standing there while he broke off a piece of the biscuit and put it into his mouth. Suddenly, I caught a closer look at the tall, blue-eyed man with sandy blond hair and a dimple in his chin while he stood before me on the porch. It was Corporal Heath Callahan.

I must admit that I almost didn't recognize him in his soiled uniform and disheveled appearance at that very moment. When he spoke, at that instant, I knew that particular voice. I asked the young corporal how he came to be back in this part of town. He told me that the Porter Guards had been dispatched back into town as a back-up unit, and that he would be stationed nearby. I could tell that he wanted to talk, but I had to quickly dismiss that thought, while at the moment my family required my immediate attention. He kindly thanked me for the water, and before he left, I promised that I would find him and we could talk later that afternoon.

Several hours later as I stood to look out the kitchen window, I saw the young corporal posted across the street. While Mama lay napping, I slipped from the house to go outside to meet and talk to him. He greeted me with a smile and told me why he was positioned there on the street. I was deeply saddened to hear what he had to say that day.

Following his departure from town, two weeks ago the Porter Guards were ordered to aid in the formation of a new defense line. The strategy behind this movement was to try to stop the Confederate forces while they made their approach on the Emmitsburg Road. He told me that his buddy Jake had been severely wounded and taken prisoner while their friend Harry was shot and killed. Corporal Callahan had barely escaped while the Guard was ordered to retreat back into the woods. He felt fortunate to have made it to safety without a scratch.

I asked if he could tell me what's happening

now. Everyone is on edge, frightened, and worried about all the shelling and cannon fire all around. I wasn't surprised when he told me that it was going to get a lot worse, and that was the reason his unit was re-positioning itself back in town. He warned me that our family, friends, and neighbors should stay inside our houses as much as possible. It was getting too dangerous to be anywhere outside. I thanked him for the warning, offered him another drink of water, and we both said our goodbyes until we could see each other once again.

It was between two and three o'clock that afternoon when Georgia's next door neighbor informed us what was presently happening nearby. Calvin McAllister told us that hundreds of Union troops were in retreat from Seminary Ridge and heading toward the south side of town. This maneuver was evidently caused by a break in the right flank which now was sending hordes of tired, fighting men through town toward our house. It wasn't long until several thirsty men were pounding at the door and begging for water. I soon found myself outside on the dusty road with my pail while I began dipping cups of water for the many soldiers who waited in line. My dress became soiled and I was drenched with sweat from the heat of the day while I ran back and forth to the well to draw more water. I couldn't stop until I was certain that all the men who waited had been given a drink. I looked to see if Corporal Callahan was near, but it was evident that he was gone. I never saw him again after that day.

Later that afternoon, around five o'clock, we received the news that additional battle lines were being formed by both the Union and Confederate armies. The Northern Army of the Potomac was being forced to retreat through town and take up new positions on Culp's Hill and Cemetery Hill. It was a shock to me when I discovered that this move put our house directly into the crosshairs and within easy rifle range. At the time, our family didn't have a clue about the unknown danger that we could possibly be facing at that very moment. All I felt that I could do was to pray for our safety and protection.

I began to feel a sense of insecurity while I watched countless Union troops on the run through the streets and alleys to escape the pursuit of the rebel soldiers following them close behind. Our once quiet and peaceful streets now erupted with the frantic noise of yelling and screaming while echoes of rifle fire were heard nearby and the boom of cannons in the far distance. I heard a Union officer on horseback yell a warning for all of us to remain in our houses and take cover or else risk being killed.

While I stood at the front door, I peeked out in time to see young Jacob Marbury while he was passing by the house. I yelled out to him and he stopped long enough to share more news with me. At the corner where Baltimore Street intersected with the Emmitsburg Road stood Snyders Wagon Hotel. About a hundred yards behind the hotel on the grounds was an apple orchard filled with a large number of trees planted on the hillside. This entire area soon began to fill with Union sharpshooters who took over the hotel and several houses.

This new line of defense was being formed on the rise to engage the line of Confederate sharpshooters who were rapidly moving into their positions as well. That was all the news that Jacob could share with me at the time while he hurried along in an attempt to reach his parent's house to check on them. So far, the McClellan house had not been chosen to have its interior and exterior used as a firing position by either force. We found ourselves suddenly trapped inside the confines of Georgia's house, and had no reason to venture outside. I tried to remain as calm as possible while I continued through the afternoon to help Mama with Georgia and the boys.

Everyone knew that across Baltimore Street on the left side, about a hundred yards from Georgia's house, there lived a tanner named John Rupp. He had a workshop located at the rear of his house. Later, I learned that he survived by simply hiding in the cellar when the rebel soldiers took over the back of the house to move in their sharpshooters. From this vantage point, it was easy to see how they could fire on the Union pickets all the way toward Solomon Welty's fence and beyond. It wasn't long until the Confederate forces occupied the land from the back of the Rupp house beyond the tannery that faced toward most of the town. The layout of the land with its higher ground proved to be an advantage to both Union and Confederate sharpshooters while the firing began and continued until dark. At times, the riflemen would seem unmerciful while many men from both sides fell severely wounded or dead in the place where they once stood. I also learned that our abandoned house on Breckenridge Street had been taken over by the Confederates who had been posted in that particular part of town. The structures that surrounded the house itself provided a clear view of the Federal position on Cemetery Hill, and also along the Emmitsburg Road.

As the day was drawing to a close, Jacob Marbury was kind enough to stop by long enough to report what he had recently learned concerning the latest developments. It seemed that the outnumbered Union forces, commanded by General George G. Meade, were finally over-powered and were presently scattered around Cemetery Hill and seeking their defensive positions while the night was closing in. It was plain to see that our house, the Wagon Hotel, and several other houses were situated on a curved arc within the new Union defensive line. Georgia's house sat dangerously close, located about fifty yards to the east of the arc, while it posed an almost perfect placement for the Union sharpshooters. Many of the dwellings in this area became secure hideouts for the Yankee marksmen while they fired on their Rebel counterparts who were seen slinking in and out of buildings around the John Rupp Tannery site, as well as other nearby houses and out-buildings. I could only imagine what the rest of the day would hold for us.

By late evening, I had come to realize that maybe Georgia's house wasn't the best place of refuge after all. Alas, we didn't have a choice now; we were all together and would have to deal with whatever was set to happen. I was determined to keep myself busy while I tried to encourage Mama and Georgia to do the same.

It wasn't long until the Confederate sharpshooters who were stationed in the Rupp Tannery on the opposite side of the street began to fire at the Union pickets positioned around our little red brick duplex house. We were now caught directly in the crossfire, and it was rapidly becoming more intense. While the rifle fire continued until dark, the bullets riveted the entire area like an unrelenting hailstorm. I looked out the front window to see a few Union soldiers who had fallen mortally wounded out in the yard and on a nearby vacant lot. When I could no longer stand it, I rushed outside to bring water and words of comfort to those men who lay wounded and dying. Later, when I returned inside the house, Mama helped me move Georgia's bed from upstairs and down into the parlor. It wasn't long until we could hear the noise upstairs of bullets passing through the bedroom walls. At bed time, a fully-dressed Mary Wade reclined on the bed with her daughter Georgia and baby Lewis, while I rested on a lounge under a window at the north side of the house. Harry slept in a trundle bed on the floor near the fireplace. Around ten o'clock that night, most of the firing had stopped around the house. The distant noises and booms from the cannons could still be heard and sometimes felt at any time. This made sleep almost impossible while the day was ending. I went to bed that night hearing the cry and moans of the wounded soldiers while they lay outside in our yard. I would get very little sleep tonight.

At first light on the morning of 2 July, the battle lines were drawn almost parallel while the main portions of both armies were in position nearly one mile apart. This awakening news was shared with us by one of the soldiers who was sheltered just outside our house. The Union forces held Cemetery Ridge while the Confederates awaited their orders on Seminary Ridge to the west. Lt. General James Longstreet's attack on the left Union flank turned the base of Little Round Top into shambles, leaving the Wheatfield strewn with the wounded and dead, while it overran the Peach Orchard. The Confederacy was the first to start up the battle on Thursday morning, this second day while the rifle firing began once again ripping up and down Baltimore Street.

The bodies of the wounded and dead lay strewn along the street, porches, doorways, and alleys at the rising of the sun. This same Union soldier who was stationed on the north perimeter of the house told me that he estimated at least 150 bullets had already penetrated our residence and outbuildings. So far, the house itself had not been the target of artillery, but it continuously worried us all since we felt entirely helpless while a new day began.

Suddenly, the familiar sound of the bullets striking the outside walls were interrupted by the crash of a misdirected ten pounder Parrot shell, probably fired from Oak Ridge, about two miles away. The blast from the screaming shell burst through the slant of the roof over the stairway on the north side of our house. It passed through the wooden shingles, and I thought it possibly plowed through the plaster walls upstairs. The impact shook the house like an earthquake, while the shell finally came to rest above the outside extension of the roof where it lodged itself. Mama and my sister became frantic as they braced themselves for the next moment of silence while they waited for the shell to explode and possibly kill us all. Praise be to God! It never exploded.

After hearing the crash of falling bricks, the splintering of wood, and plaster falling down from the walls and ceilings upstairs, Mama told me later that I had fainted and fell onto the floor. When I came back to my senses, I was laying across Georgia's bed and felt relieved to learn that the shell never exploded and we all remained safe, at least for the moment. I had to go upstairs and check on our present situation to ease my own mind. After crawling through all the debris scattered around Georgia's bedroom, I found the shell lodged in the rafters above my head. It still felt warm to the touch while I hesitantly lifted my hand to satisfy my curiosity. I prayed once more that we would all remain safe while I returned downstairs to share my findings with Mama and Georgia.

Later that afternoon, I went out into the yard to offer water and slices of freshly baked bread to the soldiers stationed around the house. The erratic firing in the neighborhood continued all during the day, but I felt that I needed to stay busy and try to bring comfort to the men who lay around the house and in the yard. I had no time to worry or fret about my own safety while we kept the stove fired up for baking. By nightfall, Mama realized that we needed to start more yeast to be mixed into the dough where it could rise and be ready for baking by early morning. That was the last task before I tried to settle down for the night and get some rest.

Around 4:30 a.m. the next morning, 3 July, Harry helped me to bring in enough wood to start up the stove while we cautiously slipped outside to the wood pile. I checked the dough tray and found that the dough had risen nicely. It looked ready for baking as soon as the oven was hot. Mama was just waking up to find

Georgia already up with baby Lewis. I started the fire and then returned to my lounge to read the Bible and have my morning devotion. All I could think about was the three men in my life who meant so much to me: my eldest brother, my brother-in-law, and the man I truly loved with all my heart.

Shortly after seven o'clock, all the windows on the north side of the house came under fire by the Rebel sharpshooters. Within a few seconds, all the panes were shattered while fragments of glass sprayed into the room and onto the floor. One stray bullet entered the front room, struck the bedpost, hit the wall, and fell onto the pillow at the foot of the bed where Georgia and her baby lay resting. She was shaken quite a bit, but felt it was a miracle that had saved her and Lewis. We all rejoiced over that while trying to regain our composure.

The clock on the mantel had just chimed eight times when I took my usual position in front of the dough board and tray. I felt that I was running late since I had promised a soldier last night that I would have a batch of biscuits ready baked early this Friday morning. Hurriedly, I sifted the flour and began to knead the mixture into the dough. While I dipped a little more flour onto my hands, I asked Mama, who stood at my side, to check the stove.

A lone rifle shot rang out...

11:14 a.m.
Trussville, Alabama
20 March 2023

References

History of a Free People
Henry W. Bragdon & Samuel P. McCutchen
The Macmillan Company
New York 1964

Wikipedia Encyclopedia 2021
Jennie Wade

Gettysburg – The Story of
the Battle with Maps
Stockpole Books
Mechanicsburg, PA 2013

Jennie Wade of Gettysburg
Cindy L. Small
Gettysburg Publishing 2017

Printed in the United States
by Baker & Taylor Publisher Services